THE GOD BEHIND THE WINDOW

THE
SEAGULL
LIBRARY OF
GERMAN
LITERATURE

MICHÆL
KRÜGER

The
God
behind
the
Window

TRANSLATED BY
KAREN LEEDER AND PETER THOMPSON

LONDON NEW YORK CALCUTTA

This publication has been supported by a grant
from the Goethe-Institut India

Seagull Books, 2022

ISBN   978 0 8574 2 998 8

British Library Cataloguing-in-Publication Data
A catalogue record for this book is available from the British Library

Typeset by Seagull Books, Calcutta, India
Printed and bound by WordsWorth India, New Delhi, India

CONTENTS

'I have nothing which I might call my own'

Hölderlin, *Hyperion*

FAREWELL

On the day his last letter arrived, just a card tucked inside an envelope, I was standing at the window after an almost sleepless night, gazing at the apple tree just beginning to blossom in the front garden. These are the three or four days of the year that, despite the pretty much constant rain, I value more than any others. Forlornly one surveys a depleted world while the old tree stubbornly puts out one flower after another from its ravaged limbs. Every year I beg that this capacity for hardship be preserved, because one can see what effort it costs the tree once again to act as if it can keep up with the saplings in the neighbourhood, already standing proudly in full bloom.

A light breeze blew up, lifting some leaves with its narrow hand and sending others others downwards before they all whirled back to rest. It's like an exercise for your core muscles, I thought. Since people have begun talking about the possibility of bees being wiped out by an unknown virus, I have been looking out of the window every morning to see whether they will grant me the honour of spending their last days in my tree. But they were nowhere to be seen. The other trees were much too attractive. I could only see the effects of this strange wind, and the leaves turning this way and that as if obeying its every whim. I had often intended to prune the tree—there was a lot of dead wood in its crooked branches, and some of the twigs were dying—but I always put it off for another year. My wariness about touching the old tree was the subject of an inner debate every morning. Veneration, shame, wanting to trim a holy thing according to one's desires—and what could be more holy than an old apple tree in blossom—laziness, or, worse, indifference; because in truth the tree was in desperate need of pruning. In recent years, I have not picked a single apple, only collected those lying in the grass, and, because the tree is so old and stubborn and exhausted, almost all the apples end up lying in the grass by summer's close. Just a few stay on the tree, right up in the crown where the birds can easily reach them, if they didn't ignore them, and some try and cling to their branches right through the winter. My apples do not taste particularly good: they are neither juicy nor sweet, and sometimes I bite into one only so that they aren't left entirely unattended, and then immediately feel bad when I throw it away.

In the summer I sit beneath the tree with my coffee and read for an hour before work. Life loses much of its gravity if, on waking, one wears all one's unresolved dreams on one's face and sits beneath a tree and reads. I used to be one of those people who first went to the bathroom to check in the mirror if I still recognized myself and to restore the face that had settled on my real one overnight. I have stopped doing that now. I have also stopped shaving, so that I no longer have to witness the grimaces I make while trying to get to the hairs in the creases. Sometimes, covered in shaving foam, I would stare at my face for long minutes, as if I could longer believe my eyes. Who are you, I would ask myself, the man looking out of the mirror, or the one staring at it? I found it impossible to accept that we were one and the same. On one side a man who still feels young and is about to leave for work, on the other a man with death in his face.

I am the business manager of a magazine company that distributes millions of more or less worthless magazines every week, and, although it is not part of our duty to know the contents of our 'product palette', my colleagues fall on the new issues in a frenzy, hoping to discover something they don't already know. This hectic flicking often takes no longer than three minutes, and you can see from their disappointed faces that it has been a waste of time. New cars, new women, new holiday paradises, new recipes but, as ever, nothing for one's own life. We are very successful: Number One in southern Germany, and, since we introduced our new computer system, we have gained more customers, most recently the leading golf journal and the top sailing magazine. As far as I know, nobody in the company plays golf or sails, but they were all beside themselves with delight at being initiated, at no cost, into the secrets of golf and sailing. Unfortunately, it is impossible for me to get excited about a new golf-club handle or golfing shoe. I remember what effort it took me to even open the magazine, how broken I felt when I was allowed—under the eagle eye of the chief editor—to close it again; and then how I called out, in a voice that didn't seem to belong to me: 'A superb product. It is an honour to be allowed to represent it.' That's when we had them. The golf magazine has one of the lowest return rates, which is also why it is much loved.

For the last year I have been reading Pascal every day, pretty much in secret, so as not to give my colleagues any reason to mock me. They consider it a mild form of idiocy for anyone to take pleasure in philosophical questions. I have made it my habit to conceal my philosophical books inside a newspaper when I take them in to read during the lunch break, so that they remain hidden from scornful eyes.

At the end of this month, my work will come to an end and the last years of my life will begin.

As I stood at the window, watching the thick buds forming on my apple tree, with cautious pleasure, a light rain began to fall, no more than a drizzle that gathered on my window pane and slowly grew until, after an agonizing wait, it began to run down the smooth glass as droplets. I was so preoccupied with this that I was only marginally aware of the postman making the strangest of gestures in order to attract my attention. But that something almost invisible (like this drizzle) could suddenly produce fat drops racing down the glass caught my attention—in any case not especially amenable to sensation on this wet Saturday morning—in a way that the wild gesticulations of the postman could not. Every Saturday he would pick up a package of magazines that he would work through over the weekend. He was the best-informed person in the world and knew everything about everyone, as far as it was mentioned in the magazines.

I went downstairs and opened the door. Since the disappearance of my wife, I occasionally forget to lock the front door; but even though I live in what people call a good neighbourhood and many of my neighbours are, quite understandably, attractive targets for burglars, I have been spared up until now. Or maybe, on seeing my library of newspaper-wrapped philosophical books, the burglars had beaten a hasty retreat.

It was only now I saw that the postman was soaking wet. He took off his yellow raincoat, pullover and shoes and followed me into the kitchen. He had put the post into the postbox already because 'I wasn't sure whether you'd even seen me, you were standing there so oblivious.' Once in the postbox, the deliveries always got wet, owing to a fault in the design of the garden gate which could apparently only be rectified by getting a completely new one. I could see the thin trickle of water running in through the gap and, drop by drop, soaking all the bills and final demands and requests to take a fuller part in society. So my visitor had to get dressed again and go and rescue the unhappy missives. That they brought misfortune I could tell from his face. Because it seems to rain more in our region than in any other part of the world, it has long been one of my most important duties each day after work to separate the wet envelopes from their equally wet contents and lay them out on the floor to dry so that I can decipher their messages. If I went away for a few days, there was no need for this almost shamanistic ritual. In that case, the letters were so soaked through, I could only retrieve them from the box as a single, soggy clump and then transfer them straight to the recycling bin. This meant that many letters went unanswered. They arrived in such a state that a proper answer was nigh impossible. However, I could never bring myself to regret the rainy-day losses because what arrived on dry days was more than enough to satisfy my need for attention. I had got rid of my email account—a present from my company on the occasion of my 60th birthday—because it had become clogged with electronic messages; and being the helpless recipient of so many unwanted approaches had a bad effect on my spiritual balance. Bit by bit, one becomes a different person if one enters into this pact with the devil. I still recall how I used to switch on the machine every morning, my hands shaking, and listen to its enterprising hum as it loaded up happily. Then came the collapse into deep depression when, at 6 a.m., an offer would already be waiting for me from Chicago, to take my place at an imaginary card table; from Hong Kong, to agree to have my penis enlarged; and from Kenya, to become rich beyond measure. My impotence worried me at first, then unsettled me and finally made me angry. By the time one had translated this neo-English pidgin into something halfway comprehensible, hours would have passed and, in the end, when everything had been moved into the recycle bin—which was never emptied—one felt so despondent, humiliated and empty that one was no longer capable of answering the few personal messages in correct German. So these too ended up in the greedy bin. And then, in the evening, the terrible realization that it would perhaps have been polite to at least thank the person for sending the message, even if one had to ask for understanding, etc. And so I would start grubbing around in the electronic rubbish bin like an old tramp; and when I did finally find the few sentences I was looking for, I was too exhausted to formulate an elegant and persuasive response. For this reason, I felt a profound sense of relief on the day I finally found the inner strength to get rid of my electronic torturer, and, to prevent myself ever weakening, decided on the spot, and with some joy, to throw it out of the window—hard disk, printer, the whole kit and caboodle—where it lay for a week in the rain on the stone path. It was only when we had a rain-free day and I decided to mow the lawn that I took them and buried them in the recycling bin between two clumps of grass. With what inner rejoicing did I return to my Pascal!

There is still the problem of the newspapers. Before six o'clock every morning, six newspapers arrive in the postbox—three German, and three foreign ones that I read in order to keep my languages up. If I fetch them from the box by seven on a rainy day, which means every second day, I can only read them in the evenings after they have dried out, except on a Saturday. If there is heavy rain or a thunderstorm, the print on the outer pages is so smeared that it is illegible and I have to confine myself to the local news and the sports section. Of course, I have often discussed replacing my heavy metal door with the supplier who has a workshop in Braunschweig, God knows why, only to be told that the hedge to the right and left of the door would need to be replaced, not to mention the cables that go under the stone slabs. Time and again he has recommended more or less explicitly that I pull down what he sees as an unappealing and impossibly impractical house so that he can build me a modern, well-insulated 'super house' that will last me 'the rest of my days' and whose postbox, 'incidentally', would stay dry in any wind or adverse weather. Fed up with this discussion, I constructed my own little wooden roof to go over the top of the massive gate but I had to take it down again when it became clear that anyone opening the door too vigorously would injure themselves. And so I was, and remain, stuck with wet newspapers. On the other hand, I recently noted something in Montaigne: 'he who observes himself properly will never find himself in the same state of mind twice.' So there is hope that I shall be able to solve this problem one day, perhaps when I manage to see it from a different perspective. For good reason we have deceived ourselves about the progress of world history which runs neither in a straight line, nor in a zigzag, but in a series of pitiless leaps. It is therefore also fitting that we are not able to determine the course of our own lives, despite the invention of grace and justice, despite regret and contrition, despite all the rules of Christianity, for it is simply not to be reckoned. Let the newspapers soak up the water. Being is the horror.

I made the soaking-wet postman an espresso, a double, on my automatic Lavazza machine. As he has only one client after me, a timid professor of education with an esoteric air who lives on his own with two cats and is happy if he doesn't receive any post from angry parents, the postman was able to linger in my kitchen and function as a living newspaper while drinking his coffee, with no official consequences. Because he was a clever man, he always found it easy to draw conclusions about what was going on. Of the daily letters received by Mr Eberhard—my arch-enemy in the street—from the tax office he was able to say: 'Mr Eberhard has more of a past than a future, even though he is twenty years younger than you.' The postman only had to take a letter between his thumb and forefinger to be able to predict the fate of its addressee. Mostly it was bad news he could sense which, according to him, had nothing to do with any special aptitude for misfortune but rather—and he could talk about this for hours— with the post itself. If only we could undo all the misfortune arriving by post, Europe, he reckoned, would be a happier place. 'Just think about the millions of obituaries that have been distributed in the twentieth century! The tax office! Advertising! People are the objects of suggestion, they attract misfortune by post—and I am the bearer of bad news!' He was of the opinion that thelittle good news that still existed was increasingly communicated by telephone, from the large lottery win to the inspirational idea, with the result that the daily misfortune he had to deliver weighed even more heavily. 'Coldness and greed, that's what I carry about every day.' I liked his pessimism (that challenged me to try and see something positive in our existence which was hard enough) as well as his pragmatism, from which the whole building profited. If he kept up his curses long enough, I began to breathe more freely. But most of all I admired his ability to read letters through their envelopes. 'If a love letter finds its way into my hand once a month, my fingers twitch like a divining rod.' He could also say with equal certainty if a farewell lay within.

We had known each other for eight years since the—unexpected—disappearance of my wife. Since then, I've lived alone in the old house. The many echoes that she left behind constantly plague me and sometimes I am close to sliding into an unequivocally pathological condition myself. As long as I knew her, she had suffered from sudden attacks of depression that were so extreme that she had to stop work in her art gallery, and it was these bouts that interrupted our daily life. And then her disappearance, out of the blue, on a rainless day in June eight years ago. Sometimes, when I return home, I see her shadow flit across the wall and can understand the things she said to me. And, of course, all her clothes are still in the wardrobe and her coats in the downstairs cloakroom; and when it rains I sometimes touch them to check whether they are wet. And sometimes I see the expression of weariness on her face when I have been talking for too long and too pedantically about the book I'm reading. It is one thing to read philosophy, but it can be a torment to go over and over the ideas without any conclusions coming to light. If everything the philosophers say about human beings were to come true, she used to say, then we wouldn't exist any longer.

The catalogue of Rembrandt's self-portraits she was looking at when she disappeared still lay open on her desk, and, when I had nothing else to do, I would sometimes sit in her chair and look at the pictures. What can move a person to paint themselves over and over again, just in order to confirm that each time a different person appears on the canvas? What is missing is the final picture, painted at the very moment of death, which could correct the impression given by all the previous pictures. Rembrandt looked at me, not the other way round. He looked at me so searchingly that I leapt up from my chair and had to get away.

The postman, who has gradually turned from an acquaintance into a distant friend, comes to visit every Saturday if I am not away, for a few hours, to check that everything is OK. He looks around the house and the garden and, sometimes, if he has time, will even cook something. He doesn't want to have a key but knows where to find it in the garage—just in case, as he says—and we all know what he means by that.

There was nothing to do today. He checked the oil level, repaired the toaster, pumped up the bicycle tyres and then came back to me in the kitchen where I was staring out of the window, the sealed letter still in my hands. Naturally he knew what was inside—I could read it in his eyes.

To distract me, he began to tell me how the woman from No. 12 had been let out of prison early.

Branded a child-murderer, this woman always maintained her innocence regarding the death of her daughter, and has now found her way back to us. It must be three years since I last saw her. The sentence was five years but obviously they had reconsidered. 'The Eyes of a Murderer' wrote one tabloid newspaper whose name I do not want to mention, and printed an image of a pair of eyes under which could have stood 'The Eyes of a Nobel Prize Winner' or 'The Eyes of a State Prosecutor'.

In fact, what should have been printed was 'The Eyes of a Desperately Sad Mother', or simply: 'The Eyes of a Mother'. But these gangsters who pretend to be journalists and unload their wagonloads of shit onto the country every day, these criminals who are accepted by society and feared by politicians, had cut a pair of deeply troubled eyes from the drawn face, two dark holes through which misery must have slid into her body, and printed underneath in bold type: 'The Eyes of a Murderer'. I was so angry about the   way these shit-shovellers had treated a defenceless human being that I went around the neighbourhood tearing down the posters, stealing all the newspapers and throwing them in the rubbish. If all the defenceless people in Germany were to take these so-called newspapers and throw them in the rubbish every day, perhaps the owners would take pity. But the opposite is the case. It is precisely the defenceless, mocked every day by these so-called newspapers, who read them and obviously enjoy being mocked; and it is the politicians who, for fear of these newspapers, shit themselves in parliament and publish their every thought in these same newspapers or say a few words that can be used by the gangsters who pretend to be journalists, as advertising. I made a mental note to find this woman or to invite her over but was sure at the same time that I would never do it.

So now his last message lay before me—this crumpled card in an envelope—the last message from my brother Hans who was not my brother.

I last saw him on a Sunday in August 2008. He came to borrow some shoelaces. I tore open the door with a threatening face because I had no intention of tolerating a disturbance so early in the morning; I had indeed rushed to the door and was ready to run through my front garden and onto the street to catch the miscreant—after God knows how many disturbances in the previous months—but there he stood, taking me and my anger in and asking about brown shoelaces.

We went down into my cellar—to be precise, into what I call my cave because, besides the wine, I used the four parts of it to store all the papers and books that could ever be used against me at any point—on that beautiful but somewhat cool Sunday in August, to find brown shoelaces. I offered him black shoelaces, but he insisted on brown. Good thick ones if possible, because he needed them for his climbing boots. He had quite strange and very particular objections to the thin shoelaces 'on offer at the moment', as he put it, because, he claimed, they were no longer made out of a single piece but from a thin, threadlike inner lace within a somewhat stronger outer coating. If the outer coating is broken, you can forget about the lace, he said, stony-faced while we inspected the laces in my shoes. Equally, his basic faith in all modern commodities was not particularly pronounced. All commodities, to generalize his oft-expressed opinion over the years, were only produced in order to promote China's efforts to become a world power. Where in Europe, he cried, have you seen a factory producing shoelaces the old-fashioned way? He whipped himself into such a fury talking about our worthless shoelaces that he succeeded in painting a picture of the futility and decrepitude of our entire continent while praising the canny Chinese to high heaven because their monopoly in the shoelace industry was forcing us to buy new shoelaces every month while European shoelaces—just think of Budapest, once the pinnacle of this industry—would last for a lifetime. It would not have speeded up our painstaking search if I had tried to talk to him in a matter-of-fact way about the problem. He wanted to be right and to be seen to be right. Always.

Once we had pulled all the halfway-decent brown laces out of their eyelets, we returned the shoes, looking rather forlorn, to their places. I will never wear them again, it suddenly occurred to me. I will never again pull a shoelace through these eyelets and put these shoes on. We had made the shoes worthless and it was only now that they looked like real shoes, but abandoned, no longer used; if Hans hadn't been there I would have taken them upstairs and thrown them in the rubbish. But as if Hans had guessed my ominous thoughts, he said—hopefully unaware that he would never again knock on my door—that when he returned from his trip, he would buy new shoelaces and make the shoes look 'respectable' again.

He didn't want a cup of coffee.

He stood there in my kitchen, his large face speckled with liver spots, his protruding ears, the shoelaces in his left hand and his right curled into a claw in the top right corner of the door frame.

What else?

I don't want to read this news any more, he said and pointed with his foot to the newspaper I had laid out across the other kitchen chair. Never again. Then he muttered goodbye, turned and disappeared.

I remember that I picked up the newspaper, one I had already read, and checked to see what the headlines were. In this case he was right. It was all about murder and death, about presidents who had gone mad in the Caucasus and in Moscow, about hijackings and kidnappings, about soldiers who had trodden on mines, about economic crises, about mudslinging in the theatre and an old man who had got stuck in Bayreuth and couldn't let go, not to mention a natural world that was pained to the quick and was plaguing the planet with murderous storms in revenge. I hadn't noticed on my first reading that the newspaper exclusively contained news and commentary designed to make one afraid. I had registered the stories individually, I guess, but not in their totality. That presidents went mad was not particularly unusual; that old men didn't want to let go is a well-known fact; that the theatre has become a mud bath was not news to anyone; and that budgets could not be balanced was already clear to every schoolchild: even though we are paying ever-more tax, we are always depriving someone of something: to pay means to steal.

I could understand that he didn't want to read this kind of news any more, but with what determination he would turn his resolution into action was not clear to me. Hans was one of those people who reacted, who exhibited reflexes, had opinions; he didn't take the lead but responded, and complained about progress, or rather about the relentless advance of progress, the course of which one could no longer illustrate with neat geometric figures but a dismal zigzag, confusion, a chaotic back and forth. But, overall, this movement was always forward and one was always left behind, breathless. And sometimes progress would turn for a second and look into the faces of those left behind, flushed and worn out by having to run so fast to keep up, as if it had never seen anything so ugly.

At home, the silence about how he had come into our family was so deafening that we children very quickly came to the conclusion that we should not talk about it. We didn't even discuss exactly when it was that he joined our family, because he was already there when I moved in, having been brought up by my grandparents. And as my brothers and sisters showed no inclination to clear up the mystery of the unexpected guest, I soon stopped asking. In any case, I was not really considered worthy of initiation into the deeper family secrets. I was treated like an object that could be engaged strategically when needed, but which, for the most part, had a particular place in the corner of the living room where it was meant to stay, unnoticed. My sisters used me as a message boy for their first love affairs, a mission I was happy to undertake because the awkward lovers would understand I was in the know and treat me politely, albeit with a good-humoured irony that I found shaming. Despite my success as a go-between for affairs of the heart, who managed to circumvent the strict moral codes of our parents, my status remained precarious. In the family hier-archy, I was right at the bottom. Hans was far above me, even though, strictly speaking, his place was outside the family.

My parents only spoke to me when necessary. All their energy was exhausted by organizing our daily life within the burgeoning economic miracle, and in the evenings they were far too tired to even listen to my questions. We'll talk about it later, was the usual answer, a leitmotif throughout my childhood. I'm not trying to say that my childhood was completely joyless. On the contrary, I felt that I was excluded in quite a neutral way and imagined that being ignored gave me a special ability to see through things.

At the weekends I would confine myself to sitting in my corner because the family had dedicated itself to sport in a singular, almost fanatical way that I found deeply repellent. Any anguish that should befall us—and alongside the unhappy love affairs of my sisters was a whole catalogue of such misfortunes—would be thoroughly expunged at the weekend with dodgeball, canoeing and hockey. I was no doubt dimly aware that this burning desire to throw balls, paddle a canoe or chase after a tiny little ball was a sign of immaturity, but I was not able to express it yet. Naturally, it was also a sign of this immaturity that nobody would speak about Hans' origins while it was a shining symbol of his own maturity that he himself never spoke about them either. Either he was in the know and had been told to keep quiet, or he knew nothing and did not wish to put this ignorance on show.

But when the family was sitting around the dining table in the evening, one could see from their glowing faces that anything that might disturb their happy lives had been wiped away. They would talk about personal bests, goals they had scored and other heroic deeds such that one might have presumed there were only winners in sport.

It was only Hans who kept us completely in the dark about his sporting preferences, even when he disappeared on Saturdays with his rucksack and returned on Sundays as if nothing had happened. It couldn't have been a team sport because Hans, to put it carefully, did not exactly like people. He avoided touching anyone if he could, a habit that he maintained into old age. He would only shake hands if he absolutely had to, which led to embarrassing situations where a person's hand was left hovering in the air, and only grabbed at the very moment the person decided to withdraw. If he was in a crowded room in a pub and had to leave, he would have preferred to flee in a single bound above the heads of the people and tables, but, because he didn't have this particular ability, he was forced to bark like an aggressive dog in order to part the crowds. When I think back, I never actually saw him embrace my mother or father and only observed the clumsiest attempt on their part to embrace him. No sooner had my mother ambushed him from behind and put her arms round him than Hans would fall to the floor; and once when my father wanted to congratulate him on receiving a medal from the German Society for the Protection of Animals for rescuing a dog, the hand that was supposed to clap him on the shoulder met only thin air. I belong to a generation that has never seen its parents undressed and we did everything we could to avoid them seeing us too. This makes one incident I do recall especially embarrassing. One day Hans was limping and, when all our questions had been stonewalled with the retort that he had injured himself at sports, my father decided on a surprise attack: he held the flailing Hans down on the sofa in front of my assembled brothers and sisters while my mother impassively and with a single tug, pulled his pyjama trousers down to his ankles. And we saw a boil as big as an egg on his hip that had to be operated on immediately. I will never forget the fascination with which my sisters bent over the taut, blue patch of skin while getting an eyeful of whatever they could. What a terrible sight! A whole family had lost its senses. On the other hand, Hans was saved: if the boil had carried on growing and burst, I would have had one fewer brother who was not my brother.

Whenever my father asked Hans how the match had been, the answer was generally: we won—as if that gave all the information that was necessary about his activity. If I was asked the same question, I would mumble some sort of lie, and, since nobody expected a substantive answer from me with regard to questions of sport, they were happy enough with that response which, moreover, my father, more often than not, answered for his part with a sigh, saying he hoped I hadn't let the family down. But if there should be some absentminded confusion and I were to be asked again how I had done, Hans always answered for me, saying that I had been with him and that was enough for them.

It was through tiny incidents like these that I gleaned that Hans was on my side without it ever having to be discussed. It sounds like an exaggeration if I say that Hans was the only person in the world that I could rely on. Perhaps that is saying too much. In fact, the people I completely trusted were my grandparents, but they lived in a part of Germany that could only be reached by post and all I could say in my letters was that I was well and with a little more work I would successfully complete the school year. I was not able to develop a relationship with the people in my class that would be worthy of the term friendship. They were alien to me; some of them so alien that I could only stare at them blankly.

Hans, on the other hand, was loyal to me when I came home from school with catastrophic marks; he defended me against my brothers and sisters whose demands I was not able to fulfil, and took the blame if I had made some sort of mess. It was part of our unofficial alliance that I never asked him where he came from and what fate—a word that I loved back then and used as often as possible—had brought him into our family.

Once I had left school, I seldom saw my family but never got the impression that this separation bothered them. My sisters married into money but became unhappy; my brothers married into poverty and became rich when our father left the family firm to them—which they made into a global pharmaceutical concern and later sold to one of their American competitors. Against the will of their wives who loved painting, they collected conceptual and minimalist art in huge quantities, and, when they thought they had enough, then forced the mayor of their town in the West, where they lived in their enormous villas, to build and maintain a museum for them even though, by that time, no one was interested in the subtleties of that sort of art any more. I once visited the museum, after my brothers had died, one morning in March and was the only visitor, apart from the museum attendants sitting there to guard the thin brush-strokes. I remember that I was embarrassed to show the free pass my brothers had given to me on one of my significant birthdays, because I was afraid that I would be recognized as a member of the family and made responsible for the disaster. I ordered a piece of cheesecake in the cafe and was told by the bored staff that they were about to throw it away because it had been hanging about for days.

I had not been offered a place in my father's firm. Of course, I never made any secret of the fact that I could muster no special enthusiasm for the production and distribution of painkillers but was nevertheless surprised by how easily they could ignore me, even my mother, as if I were neither entitled to, nor capable of, taking part in family decisions. I felt no sense of reproach towards my parents and still do not, but the astonishment that they trusted my brothers completely but me not is still with me. I got my due, of course. After a degree in business studies, sometimes bordering on imbecility, I took various dead-end jobs with no great enthusiasm until I ended up at a big newspaper and stuck with it. Whether this was out of laziness or lack of imagination, I cannot say.

When, on the death of our parents, my brothers and sisters asked me to choose a few pieces of furniture or plates and vases to remember them by, I declined. I left behind all the things from my childhood too. Except for one photograph: of the family on holiday on the island of Sylt, but not me. I was missing for some reason that I can't remember. It shows a family that had made something of itself in post-war Germany. A colour photograph; in the background, the sea is glittering as if it belongs to this happy group of people. Sometimes

I look at the photograph, held captive in a silver frame and positioned in front of the complete works of Thomas Mann on my bookshelves. The family seems almost to quiver with energy; only my mother is making an unhappy face, as if she cannot imagine how she will escape in one piece. Hans is pointedly looking down at his naked feet. I have never been a fan of photo albums and never taken photographs myself; photographs of me do nevertheless exist, unfortunately, though I am of the opinion that there are too many in the world and they do not make it a more habitable place.

At my parents' funeral—they were blessed with a death three days apart while at their Spanish property, and the police were satisfied that it was due to natural causes—my brothers first mentioned the rumour that my father had been a member of the Waffen-SS and taken part in mass executions in Poland. A crumpled photo was passed around the circle of astonished relations, in which a man in uniform could be seen but without the slightest resemblance to my father. The man was wearing a helmet and a pair of glasses and only the SS emblem could be seen clearly. The photo was passed from hand to hand, in silence, as if everyone were aware of the shadow that had fallen across the family, apart from one sister-in-law who was known for her cheery constitution and who said with great conviction: a dashing young man! With that, some of those who didn't know us very well thought that the matter was closed. But it was immediately clear to me that this public revelation on the part of my brothers—who had, after all, made themselves rich on my father's money—was directed at Hans, our non-brother, who, thank God, was not present.

Hans became a philosopher, even if he always objected to the title. Even during his time as a student he published essays in the opinion-forming magazines of the day on questions of art and theatre, on the reform of the reform of the school reforms. He wrote and published his dissertation on Kierkegaard and was made a professor on the publication of his almost thousand-page study of Schelling's philosophy of art. He had spent months looking through the philosopher's papers and wrote some very funny Feuilleton pieces on the life of a filing card, but he never took up a job at a university. He was a guest professor in many countries, and, because he had an aptitude for languages, could choose where to hold lectures and name his fee. He wrote entries in artists' catalogues, translated Catullus and Horace and, if he had spare time during all this activity designed to prolong his lifespan, wrote stories in which he always gave himself a hard time.

I've never had any inclination to take up more room on the planet than was due to me and Hans, too, was anything but a braggart who went about the place self-aggrandizing; but his writing, his ideas, needed ever-more space to be able to develop. He wanted to expunge any sort of illusion from his thinking and so felt the need to explain things over and over until he was satisfied, or at least got close to understanding the original concept. In other words, he was obsessed with writing; he would have liked nothing better to have turned himself into a text in the end. Everything else was secondary.

In the 1960s we bought a piece of land on a Yugoslavian island near Dubrovnik through intermediaries he met at a philosophy conference. Hans wanted to learn to play the flute and needed as few neighbours as possible. In the mornings, I would work on my pathetic project on some vital statistical conundrum or other, while he got on with his philosophical exercises. In the afternoons, I worked on renovating the house, which was in a state of total disrepair, while he busied himself with mathematical problems, and in the evenings, when I was moved to tears by the miracle of the sunset, he worked on the oral traditions of the Balkan epic. His talent for languages and interest in dialects meant that all sorts of linguists fetched up in our garden to discuss all manner of strange vowel shifts. Nobody knew how they found us. It was part of Hans' peculiar magnetism that people were drawn to him in the strangest way. Even though he did everything he could to avoid contact, he could not escape.

I also looked after the animals: the donkeys that came with the property and those we acquired there: a dozen goats that Hans worshipped because they completely ignored him at first and only gradually, as his flute playing improved, sought out his company. There were also chickens, ducks and geese. But the main attraction was two pigs: huge, sturdy beasts that lay around all day in the dirt and only moved in the evenings when they had to be tied up—to stop them, in their grunting tenacity, from digging up and destroying our freshly planted garden. Only he who has lived among pigs . . . Thus began one of his essays, on pigs in ancient mythology. It was dedicated to our pigs.

The only manual activity that was left entirely to Hans was the rebuilding of the stone wall around our property. It had collapsed in several places and was in a desolate condition in general because, over the years, the larger stones had been stolen with no regard to the smaller ones that then came tumbling down. Hans travelled the length and breadth of the island in our neighbour's lorry in order to buy (or steal) new stones which he would then fit into the wall with endless care and a good deal of theory. The wall became the symbol for his philosophy. There were the large stones supporting everything and the small ones that fit into the gaps; the round ones that everyone likes; the pointed ones that everyone needs; the colourful ones that take some finding; and the grey ones that represent only themselves. Each stone was carried around until it found its rightful place in this marvellous wall, made completely without mortar in the old way since people first decided to separate their land from that of their neighbours. Each stone must have the feeling that it contributes to the stability of the whole, he would cry, after he had completed another metre. It was his firm conviction that, once in their lives, everyone should do something like this—something with one's own hands—in order to earn the name philosopher. Otherwise we might as well just use barbed wire like all the other idiots, philosophers included, who rule the world.

The unification of contradictions into a seamless whole is perhaps how one might best describe this project that Hans worked on for three long summers. Then suddenly the stony guest was complete and surrounded our house, not as a square paddock but following the contours of the land and with a slight curvature to it, so that only we—and the goats, if they stood on their hind legs—could see the land around us.

The inauguration of our reduction—as Hans called our fortress, in good Jesuit manner—was celebrated with a meal to which the neighbourhood was invited. They sat on old fruit boxes and listened to a speech by Hans, in Serbo-Croat naturally, and one could tell from the salvo of laughs that they were pleased with this strange patron saint, and even our animals appeared to think it only fitting to be living in a fenced-off world.

In the coming years, I would travel to our house over Easter and in the summer holidays and once more for Christmas, as I did not want to leave it standing empty for long. I would look after the garden and was as happy as a little boy when I succeeded in producing home-grown tomatoes and courgettes for my supper. When I was alone, I would go for long walks, focusing only on the movement of my legs, or sit by the sea and observe the waves as if this absence of activity was the very point of my existence. We had the most beautiful sunsets, and nothing was more moving than the moment when the sun sank down behind the shining metallic surface of the sea. At night, I would read Ivo Andrić or Jara Ribnikar or Vasko Popa's wolf poems, and when the wind blew up and forced the smoke back down the chimney into the room, I would set a chair in the open doorway and stare into the darkness. I could imagine no other or better life, and, when I eventually brought a gramophone to the island, my happiness in being alone was complete. My heart opened in the way a fist opens after a fight.

Of course there was no stopping my paradise catching the eye of the devil. Hans had developed the habit of turning the house more and more into a sort of seminar every summer. Young people he had got to know, God knows where, were invited to come and philosophize with him for a few weeks, and soon there came professors from Belgrade who were having difficulties with the Party, Statists and Trotskyists—who often hated one another's guts—and wished to present their ideals about the correct form of the state to various open-minded socialists from the West. What is the State? Nothing less was worth discussing.

For a small charge the guests would sleep at our neighbours' houses or in tents and I was responsible for looking after them. To be honest, I hardly understood a word of what was being discussed, so that soon I was treated like a waiter vaguely interested in matters of philosophy. What was a just State? What was the role of the Party? I had never given matters like this any thought, and the manner of their debates was not exactly conducive to my thinking more about them. It was always about the future; the present was more or less written off. I could not imagine the future as a beautiful place. My mistrust grew when, one day, a group of young French Marxists arrived who wanted in all seriousness, to start a revolution and—as a joke, as Hans later assured me—proposed that we should start with the socialization of our property. When I refused point-blank to entertain such childish plans and they learnt that I worked in the magazine world, their next demand was that we should found an international journal titled *Revolution* whose German edition I should be responsible for distributing. They couldn't even wash up properly. They shovelled the food that our neighbour Ante and I had prepared for them into their mouths without comment, drank great quantities of our wine, which they described as 'basic, but tasty', and headed down to the sea with their revolution in order to prepare themselves for the evening meal. Washing-up was left to me and Svetovar, a moderate Stalinist who, during our silent tasks, sang one communist song after another or murmured radical left-wing slogans to himself without even looking at the dishes. It was immediately clear to me that with this lot involved any revolution was doomed to failure.

Among them was a young woman with a Vietnamese background who was keen on taking on the French edition of *Revolution* and who reacted especially bitterly to my saying that I wanted to have nothing to do with the revolution, or the *Revolution*. She was very beautiful in an old-fashioned way, with smooth limbs, and when she got excited during the discussions she seemed to float above the general sense of enlightenment that the group gave off, like an angel. She said that she had written a book about apocatastasis, which one was only allowed to talk about in hushed tones, titled *God's Memory*. She had arrived with a historian, somewhat broad of beam and akin to a frog, who gloated that history would have to be rewritten after the revolution, a task he was more than happy to take on, 'along with all of you, of course,' he generously conceded. When he talked, his face turned to thunder, rain, hail, destruction. He got a very bad sunburn on his first day and glowed red as the setting sun and could neither sit nor lie down; a terrible sight. Any encounter with him was, above all, an exercise in interruption, because he had to flee into the shade of the house every few minutes. His sunburn worked in my favour because 'almond eyes', as I called the beautiful young radical, knocked on our door in the middle of the night and asked to be allowed to sleep in the house. The historian was preventing her from getting any sleep with his noise. There were two beds in opposite corners of the one ground-floor room—the upper floor was not yet completed—in which Hans and I slept. There was not a lot of choice. The philosopher had a little velvet bag with her in which she kept a handful of flat stones; she scattered them on the table and, after studying them for a long time, came to the decision that she would sleep in my bed.

She stayed with me for the eight days of the seminar, and, when a boat arrived to take the group and Hans away to attend to the next revolutionary deadline, I asked her not to leave. She stayed. We looked after the animals together; I showed her how to milk a goat and, using Marx's 18th Brumaire, taught her enough German to be able to read the classics in the original. I was thankful to her. Her name was Mitsou. From then on I slept in Hans' bed and she in mine. Before I turned out the light, she looked at me with a mixture of self-confidence and contempt.

In the autumn of that same year I decided to go to the island for a long weekend in order to prepare the house against the winter weather. Hans was in Berkeley. Twice a week I would go to his flat to sort through his post. Important letters were to be read out to him on the telephone. When I rang the number he had left for me, a male voice answered and said he had never heard of Hans. He didn't know the philosophy department's number. He was a chemist. I gave up. Hans would get in touch.

The island was particularly beautiful at the end of October. The late light made everything finer and more transparent; and only the wind, that had everything in its grasp, was a disturbance. It blew the clouds up into great sheets that seem to hang over the burnt grass. The animals lay peacefully, pressed against the walls of the house. Only the donkeys were absent, Ante was sure to have loaned them to someone. The inside of the house looked as though it had only just been abandoned and I wouldn't have been surprised if the teapot was still warm. Somebody must have been staying in the house, because the record player was showing its unblinking green eye. Mendelssohn's octet Opus 20, one of my favourite pieces, was on the turntable. Had I forgotten to turn it off?

It was Ante who told me that Hans and Mitsou had spent a week together in the house and left that very morning. He had, she said, praised the young philosopher to high heavens. Just imagine, he had cried out, she can even milk goats!

When Hans came to Munich that winter in order to change his suitcase and travel on to Bologna, I hardly recognized him. He looked so dishevelled, pale and thin. His book *The Future* had appeared in Italian translation, so he had taken up a guest professorship there where he could also freshen up his Italian. He took Mitsou with him as his assistant.

I had no idea what he had to say about the future but I told him that, henceforth, I would like to be alone on the island and so we would have to come to some arrangement. Hans looked at me, didn't say a word but I knew that he knew that I knew.

I never went back to the island. Sometimes I imagined the animals, the goats above all with their yellow-green eyes and the chickens with their scrawny necks, and scarce feathers. I heard the terrified squawking as Ante wrung their necks. None of the people who had stayed with us to discuss Hegel could slaughter a chicken. They ate the chickens. And of course I imagined Mitsou, like a noble creature, talking with the grunting pigs. A few years later she took her own life, together with the overweight historian, a French disease of the moment. Hans sent me an excerpt from *Le Monde*, no note. Hans loved obituaries. When he had found a particularly gruesome example, he often said that—when he had time—he would write a comparative study of different European obituaries.

We hardly saw each other after that. Sometimes he wrote short letters, rushed and confused, sometimes there were off-prints of essays. Once, in a postscript, he wrote: I will feel responsible for you until the end of my days. I can only discharge that responsibility properly if I don't die before you. The best thing would be if we died together.

He couldn't come to my wedding, he said, on account of teaching commitments in China; about the disappearance of my wife, whom he never met, no word.

And so we die together.

THE TREE-HUGGER

I think I know everyone living in my area still brave enough to venture out, or at least most of them. I know who has a dog and who is plagued by which illness; who goes to church on Sunday but still believes in God; whose children respect their parents and visit regularly; who suffers from a deficit of inner balance and who is overweight; who stands in league with the powers of darkness and who in the light. I know them all. In the summer, with the windows open onto the street, I can tell by the sound of their footsteps what sort of mood they are in; I can recognize them by the tickle in their throat or their self-confident cough, by their sighs and their oaths. I know the silent ones and the mistrustful ones; those who slouch along, disappointed by life; and those who hold themselves upright and stride out, but don't want to admit that they too are on their way to meet their own misfortune.

I know them all and can see right through them.

Some of them try to torture me in my dreams; others simply clench their fists in their pockets as they pass my window. No one says hello. No one looks up at my window, no one raises a hand in greeting. Some of them have come to terms with their own death, others try to tread more lightly in order to distract themselves from it. All of them appear in the book of my imagination without knowing in what way their habits and stories are intertwined there. They cannot know because I speak to no one. I am, I sometimes think, a sort of fallen god, the God behind the window who is bound to his throne by an evil twist of fate, no longer able to release himself and go out among the people. A God who can no longer intervene, who can no longer correct his creation, but whose divine ability to interpret every step has remained. It doesn't matter how perfect a mask they wear— I see the face behind it. This miserable game of hide and seek cannot deceive me.

As far as I can remember, I have never been wrong in all the time that I have had to stay behind my window. Not once. I knew when some-body's wife had run away, and who was having trouble with the tax office. And, naturally, all their various arts of disguise have not been able to pre-vent me from recognizing the tiny, unintentional gesture that marks the fall from the trajectory of my fellow citizens' lives. Meals on Wheels brings me my food every day and I am able to pass on valuable information about who will be their next customers; the ever-dwindling trickle of post is dealt with by a Polish cleaning lady; and I don't answer the telephone any more. I maintain contact with the world through the radio. It is an old-fashioned contraption and I have no difficulty picking up broadcasts from all my neighbours' houses. I only use it to keep an eye on things, and confirm my predictions, and, of course, I also listen to the news in order to give my local observations greater context. But mostly I listen to music. I think I can say that I have heard all the significant pieces of music several times.

Music keeps me alive.

There is only one person I cannot read. He shows himself as dusk begins to fall, wearing an over-large coat even in the summer and, seen from my window, looking as if he has either forgotten how to walk or is just learning. I don't see him approaching from left or right, and he does not announce himself; he just appears out of nowhere, suddenly standing there under the street lamp, quite still and resting against the lamppost as if the wind had taken hold of him. I can only see him properly when the light begins to flicker; before that he is just part of the shadows or part of the street. He only becomes a real person when he's leaning against the lamppost. Sometimes, after a long day of observation and interpretation, when I am just entering the land of dreams, the flickering of the light brings me back. That's when I see him standing there, a totally wretched figure, breathing so heavily that his large coat—maybe a cloak or a cape or an academic gown—moves slightly up and down, because this miserable man cannot breathe like the rest of us but gasps, as if it takes a colossal effort to move his cadaverous body. Sometimes he wears a beret over his thinning hair which comes down over his ears; he wears it in summer too, which doesn't improve his appearance.

Once this person has rested for a while in what would be, for anyone else, a distinctly disadvantageous position, he reflects for a moment and then scurries, with laughably short steps, towards the nearest tree. When he reaches it, he puts his arms around it tenderly but also seeking support. Something which takes only a few seconds comes across as if he were stumbling from one end of the world to the other. He falls, as it were, into the arms of the tree as if he had just crossed a desert, and his long, thin fingers wander over the bark as if he wants to identify it by touch. Can one imagine a more intimate pair?

He is the tree-hugger whom no one knows and whom I cannot interpret. Should he be lit up by the headlights of a passing car, he loosens the hand closest to the street and forms it into a fist that he shakes at the person who has dared interrupt his embrace. He can spend up to an hour like this, an hour of exchange that goes unrecorded on any clock, an hour of brotherhood or perhaps an attempt to become one with the tree.

This man, or, better, creature, who obviously has nothing left but this tree in front of my window, his flowing coat wrapped around his gasping body, leaning against the tree as if he had been whipped: an idiot or a holy fool. No one knows where he comes from. No one knows what he does all day, whether he mourns or dreams. He comes only to embrace the tree and does not know that he is being observed by me as he does so. Or maybe he knows that I am sitting behind my window and inspecting him? Is he testing me? Is he the final challenge of my final days? Is his embrace of the tree some sort of religious ritual with which he wishes to show me my own limitations?

In any case, the strange saint, as I have come to call him, throws my theories about the transparency of human beings into confusion. I had always imagined God as a being who controls us like puppets but who forces us to behave as if we were independent; hence the elaborate masks we employ to demonstrate our free will. What gave my life meaning was seeing through these disguises, a game that one can only play for its own sake, without hope of reward or indeed redemption. It is, as should be clear by now, an entirely pointless game. The tree-hugger, as he steps into the light, reminds me of my limitations when I grow vain on account of my abilities; when I think of myself as a higher being.

I am happy when he does not appear for a while. I know he will turn up again eventually. He'll be back. He does not have the heart to leave me alone behind my window.

FOREVER

Because I felt beyond help, and because the
Munich rain only deepened that sense of helpless-
ness and dark sadness, I took the manuscript I
was working on with no success at all—time
and again, I struck out sentences only to replace
them with ever-less-concise constructions—flung
it into a small travelling suitcase along with some
clean clothes and a wash-bag on top, took the
newspaper and the post from the postbox and got
into the car in the dubious hope that my despon-
dency would be dissipated by movement, although
I already knew from previous episodes that movement was the worst possible thing. If the world is
empty, all other worlds are empty too. Only peace
and quiet would help. But I had been trying for
more than a month to calm myself, had been silent
for days, did not answer the telephone, nor listened to music, did not switch on the television,
sat down early every morning at my desk, looked

at the few lines on the paper and scraped away at them—but they refused to speak to me. They just looked back at me evilly, and all my putative improvements, even the tiniest adjustment, caused them to scoff with contempt. Why couldn't I leave them alone? What demon compelled me to get closer to the truth?

I drove through the deserted streets of the city that early morning and stopped at a cafe where dustmen in their orange uniforms were warming themselves, silent Turks who drank their coffee loudly without casting a glance in my direction. Perhaps, I thought, I should give them my manuscript: then it would land along with the bottles and old newspapers, coffee grains and leftovers on the giant garbage heap that seemed to me at that moment our civilization's inevitable destination, a massive pile of refuse where all the filth of all our efforts at finding a way to live were heaped up in chaos.

All the lies about bequeathing a cleaner world to the next generation would be there too, composting with the rest, and the rain would turn this toxic brew into a gelatinous broth that no archaeologist would ever dare touch. These thoughts, which I realized to my horror were causing my eyes to twitch and then seizing my whole body in some sort of hysterical fit, did not seem to affect the Turks at all. They simply stood there, their forearms leaning on the wobbly round tables, their faces grumpy and exhausted. Some had taken off their caps, one was leaning against the wall with his legs apart and his eyes closed, the lids moving slightly as if in sleep. Rubbish! What does one dream of when one spends the whole day dealing with what other people throw away? One dreams, naturally, of being able to produce more rubbish oneself. The woman behind the counter, with tattoos on both arms running up under the body of her sleeveless blouse, observed the orange still-life before her with little enthusiasm. She didn't even say goodbye as I left, and, manuscript tucked under my arm, got back into the car.

Why on earth the Germans were afraid of these peaceful Muslims, who took away their shit every day, was beyond me. The state would collapse if they went on strike. I imagined how it would be if a law were passed requiring every individual to deal with their own rubbish; and in my mind's eye I could see the long queues of beautiful German cars with beautiful German housewives queueing up in front of the rubbish dumps. Even looking at other people's rubbish would cause envy and unhappiness. Why are they throwing away books? Because I have read them and cannot tolerate their presence any longer. And you: why don't you eat all your food? Because, quite simply, after three bites, I feel sick at having to eat the flesh of dead animals every day. I should write a

piece for the theatre, I thought, called *Rubbish*.
Rubbish is a very popular theme in contemporary
theatre. It would probably do the rounds. In my
play, however, the Turks would laugh and show
their gold teeth in their sad Anatolian faces and
stand around the stage in just the way they had
stood around in the cafe. I even had a role for the
tattooed waitress—everyone would be wondering
how the tattoos continued underneath her blouse.
That's nothing to do with you, you filthy Turks,
she would call out, and the friendly Turks would
laugh and show their gold teeth which would glint
right to the back row. At the end, there would be
a great pile of rubbish on the stage, a gigantic
stinking mountain of rubbish, and no curtain
would fall.

I had hardly turned back on to the diversion when
I saw a young man without an umbrella standing
at the side of the road, holding a scrappy card-
board sign with the word 'Innsbruck' on it. It was
clear to me in that moment that I was going to
Innsbruck. Had the sign said Paris or Barcelona, I
would have driven to Paris or Barcelona, but now
Innsbruck was going to be my goal. The young
man was so astonished that I stopped that he hesitated before bending to my open window and
murmuring 'Innsbruck?' as if he couldn't believe
his luck. Okay, let's drive to Innsbruck, I said.

I had hitchhiked around Europe in my youth and knew how sublime it felt when a driver was going to the same place you were. The young man had scarcely settled his dripping frame on the passenger seat than he introduced himself and was so ebulliently grateful that I immediately began to regret my decision to take him with me. How nice it would have been to drive to Innsbruck on my own, like a snail that had withdrawn into its shell. It is a humiliating feeling, not to be able to stand one's own loneliness and to weaken at the first opportunity. And now began the thing that I hate more than anything else: conversation. Human beings cannot, no matter how they try, keep their mouths shut. Having to entertain other people is a terrible torture. I decided not to say anything. Nothing. The young man would have to entertain me.

When I finally asked what he was intending to do in Innsbruck in this weather, I discovered that he was a theology student and that, after submitting his dissertation on the Jesuit General, St Francis Borgia, he intended to join a Jesuit college there. I gave him a sidelong glance, as I wasn't sure whether this strange, soaking-wet scarecrow was playing a practical joke, but he looked back at me without any hint of irony. He was serious. The things that young people come up with when the world is not as they wish and they see no opportunity to change it. They pray. They become pious and pray. Or they remain impious and pray for inner strength. Instead of falling into intellectual despair, like we used to, straight after their A-levels they start worrying about their eternal soul. I was probably taking one of the next popes to Innsbruck, I thought.

And then the young man began to tell me about Francis Borgia who'd apparently said, also without irony: 'like lambs have we crept into power, like wolves have we used it, like dogs shall we be driven out, but like eagles shall we renew our youth.' And when I turned off at the next service station, he took his manuscript out of his rucksack, which he had put on the back seat next to my case, and started reading out to me— until way past Rosenheim—the most perfidious accusations that had been brought against the Jesuits. Even the arch-Catholic Kaiser Franz, he shouted over the monotonous trudge of the windscreen wipers, refused to have Jesuits as Confessors and would not trust them with a parish. It was the same with Kaiser Ferdinand and the otherwise pious Ludwig of Bavaria. Maria Theresa had banned the Jesuits from her lands because they were accused of breaking the seal of the confessional. In Bologna, they were tolerated on condition that they kept themselves to themselves, which was, he said in a self-satisfied way, an impossible task. Keeping the Jesuits away from intrigue is like forbidding clear water to fish, he read from an invective launched by the Bishop of Pistoia, Scipio Ricci—a man of true piety and strict morals who lived like a saint. He is supposed to have said to Napoleon 'General! Believe me. The Jesuits are the wolves of the church and are to be feared the more so because they appear in sheep's clothing!'

This young man ensconced so happily next to me, casually listing all the suspicions that had been raised against his future order, was beginning to appear more and more sinister to me. When, under constant rainfall, we turned off onto the Inn valley motorway and I asked him to stop talking, he stopped immediately. Silent and somehow acquiescent, he looked off in the direction where one would normally be able to see mountains, even though in my current state of mind I wasn't sure that they hadn't been carried away long ago. A strange Jesuit indeed. Because this was precisely the point at which he should have started his work. I myself have never contributed much to discussions and always envied my friends who seemed able to tell the whole history of the world from a single stone or a feather as their starting point. I have always been in awe of those who were interested in theories that explain everything: psychoanalysis, gender politics, Marxism, structuralism, etc. The world became more transparent and lighter as they spoke, and I became more opaque and more heavy. But most of all I have always envied those who can fight with passion for an abstract idea, even if they know that the idea is hollow and windy, like religion. I belong with those who simply wait and see, which leads many of my increasingly rare interlocutors to believe that I am 'deeper' than, in truth, I am. I am not deep, just despairing, but of course one keeps that to oneself.

In the ensuing silence, my heart seemed to shut down. I could hear how, with the last of its strength, it swelled and pumped to keep me alive, but I could not give it my thanks. For a split second I thought that it had noticed my weariness and simply given up the ghost. I quickly came to a stop at the side of the road, put on the warning lights and, in panic, took some deep breaths. What would happen if I gave up now? Nobody would mourn the fact that I had not finished a book whose existence was only rumoured anyway; almost no one would mourn the fact that I was no longer on the earth; there were already too many people in the world and too many books setting out to explain the world to them. There was nothing more to explain. Should one explain greed again, the envy, selfishness or jealousy that have rendered the earth uninhabitable? Why not just listen to music? Why not simply spin once more but with different words that convoluted and age-old story about how human beings came to walk upright, how they could suddenly stand up and see and be seen from far away? Everything has been written, and all the theories that have been developed to understand what has been written are not worth the paper they are written on. So why turn again to Odysseus, Parsifal or Hamlet?

Well, we just have to, I heard myself mumble. It is our only chance to discover the tiny flaw in the fabric, the deviation, the hairline crack that has appeared in our story and that will one day be responsible for the break, the interruption, the end of this incredible construction of which no one who looks on in awe has ever grasped more than one per cent. One per cent, tops! But all those zealously concocting their new theories do so as if they had a decisive solution in their hands with which they can tear away the last veil from the face of grief. Only poets know better, or maybe theologians who, of course, have it easy with their one God who never feels the breath of competition on his neck.

While all this was going through my head, I felt my body suddenly grow hot and crumple like heated wax. But just before it melted away completely, I felt a stout wind pick me up and fling me through the clouds, up to a flock of birds flying effortlessly in great loops above the river Inn which now glinted in the sun as if there had never been any heavy rain; a sinuous ribbon sparkling in all colours and at whose end the churches of

Innsbruck rose up like stalks of fresh asparagus between the friendly aspect of the surrounding mountains. The flock that had incorporated me after a short initiation ritual formed itself suddenly into a narrow triangle, and we shot—the wind seemed to be tugging the skin from my bones—into a bank of clouds that rose above the little individual clouds that seemed to stand around like pieces of lost luggage. And from this amorphous mass there emerged a face—a broad, sad, astonished face—its eyes wide open. It was my face; I recognized it straight away, although my eyes were watering in the wind. There you are, I wanted to call out, but I had to give in. There was no way of breaking the strict discipline of this collective flight, and, at eye level, we flew directly into me.

I screamed myself awake. When I finally forced open my eyes, which felt as if they had been stapled shut, I found myself looking into the calm face of the would-be Jesuit who had laid me on the wet strip of grass next to the motorway and, patting me gently, had been trying to stop me flying off with the birds—were they cranes, storks or crows, white crows, angels?—to a place of irresistible infinity for me, the realm of God for him.

You're white as a sheet, he said.

A sweet, pungent smell like stables and slurry blew across from the other side of the road, and the mountain had acquired a white sash of mist that resisted the weakening rainfall. Nothing seemed to me to be as beautiful as this strip of mist and I asked myself, lying soaked on the grass in front of the Jesuit, whether it would be a bad thing to leave life with this picture in mind. Most people died in a hospital room and their last impression was the uncomfortable bed, a handful of tubes and their worried relatives. I in contrast had the sublime image of the mountains before me and a trainee priest beside me. In any case, I drank in every detail as precisely as possible, just in case, here outside Innsbruck, was really my last chance to see the beauty of the world.

As the young Jesuit neither possessed a driving licence, nor could steer the car, I sat back down in the driver's seat and drove the short distance into Innsbruck. One can die in Innsbruck just as well.

I found a room in the Grey Bear that was ideal for the way it chimed with my mood. As I entered, I was thinking about nothing else. It was dark and musty, as if I was the first guest to be given the room after many years. Indeed, I felt a sense of gratitude at not having been turned away. I hardly managed to fill out the form, my hand was shaking so much; and, under the watchful eye of the receptionist, I mixed up the answers so that the completed form looked like a spiritual message that only initiates could read. How long do you wish to stay? I was asked, and because I didn't know the answer, I said, with a dry mouth: 'Forever'.

I took the tattered manuscript, bristling with scraps of paper full of notes, from my bag and threw it onto the tiny table which, even if I had been in any fit state, would not have been suitable to work on. Having stayed in many hotels in my life, I can say that there has only been one table that really heartily welcomed me to work at it. It stands (I hope it still does) in the American Colony in Jerusalem. It had the remarkable characteristic that, during the whole day I had to spend in that dusty and noisy city, I longed to return to it. In the evening, when the others were sitting in their Armenian restaurants and bemoaning the hopeless state of the country, I was sitting at the vast, cool table, reading and writing and—forgive the pathetic word—happy. Great pain and great happiness make for pathos, something that is not always conducive to writing.

Sitting in my room in the Grey Bear, I was no longer sure what my life amounted to; what held it together; what belonged to me and only to me; of what I could say: that is mine, that is me. Even though I was careful not to expect an answer from myself, I was so keen to receive one that the contradiction gave rise to further trembling and a sadness that almost tore me apart. No book, no thought, no meditation, could liberate me from the impossible answer. Not even the thought of some of my more cynical friends who habitually tried to calm me with talk of the essentially contingent nature of each individual existence. Should I lie down? Throw myself on the floor? Scream? I didn't have the energy. So I stayed sitting on the uncomfortable chair, breathing slowly, and laid my hands, unfolded, in my lap in the unnatural way that I had been taught, and waited. Waiting seemed to me to be the only appropriate way to survive. I didn't want to wait for something, merely to wait. Someone would come along at some point to interrupt my waiting, be it life or death or just the chambermaid wishing to turn down my bed.

But where had the young Jesuit disappeared to? It was possible he might have made a good Virgil. He had disappeared along with his dissertation and his bag, as if bringing me back to life had absolved him of all responsibility. He obviously had better things to do.

After an age I switched on all the lights, including those in the hallway and the bathroom, in order to see my own shadow, at least. As long as it was moving I was still alive. My room, which was on the top floor of the hotel, did not have a balcony but there was a little sill beneath the window so that my cigarette ash blew away only after it had cooled. It was strictly forbidden to smoke in the Grey Bear. I looked down at the street for a long time and watched the cyclists who behaved as though they had everything still ahead of them. I tried to follow some of the passersby with my eyes but found I couldn't. What were they intending to do? What did they want?

The situation also had its comical side; something bitterly grotesque. I was sitting quite alone in the head of the Grey Bear in Innsbruck and had no idea what I could do to get back in touch with the story I was writing and which had abandoned me. I smoked and looked down into the depths, the tantalizing depths that held no particular attraction for me. One would probably die if one jumped, unless one happened to land on the roof of a passing car and woke up in hospital. Then you'd have to try again later.

The room was killing me, there was no doubt about that. Because the hotel restaurant was more or less empty, I went out to look for an alternative. I wanted to be among people who acknowledged my existence but did not want to talk to me. The thought of getting into a conversation with a local was paralysing because I knew how much energy it would take. At the same time, I couldn't do without people.

I found an Italian-sounding restaurant right next to the river Inn, which, because of the permanent rainfall, was doing its theatrical best to entertain the tourists with massive sheets of water thundering through the valley. The restaurant looked hopeful and, as it turned out, was run by

Croats. It was full to bursting and noisy, so noisy that the waitress had to press her hard ear against my mouth in order to hear the words gnocchi, wine and water. To show that she had understood she gave me the thumbs up. No problem, it's on its way.

Suddenly Trakl's grave came to mind: not Trakl's poetry but his grave, and I wanted to go and find it at that very moment. Why are you not lying next to Trakl? I thought. Or on his grave-stone, to warm up his bones, tormented by the cold and the rain? Surely the point was which stranger's bones one chose to enter eternity with, having spent a life with people one had met purely coincidentally? We spend our lives walking over bones. We can hear them cracking and breaking but we don't let that disturb us, even when we walk with our eyes to the ground, even when our words fall to the ground, to the thin crust of earth covering the bones. But where, in the heavy dark-ness outside, was Trakl's grave?

The owner (or perhaps the head waiter?) of the noisy restaurant had sat me at a tiny corner table so that I didn't—as he conceded quite openly—take up one of the tables for four, with my chalky white face, because today he could fill all the tables; today was his lucky day: everyone wanted to come to his restaurant. He also advised me to order the gnocchi which his mother had made that morning by hand. You won't find better gnocchi in the whole of Innsbruck, he shouted into my ear. I wanted to shout back that I hadn't come to Innsbruck to eat the best gnocchi in the city. Why was I in Innsbruck anyway? Because a young theologian had led me here?

While I picked at my food, gnocchi in puddles of ancient fat, I observed a young woman who was also sitting alone at a table opposite me and paying inordinate attention to her salad. Meticulously and joyfully, she folded each leaf into a manageable parcel, dunked it in the sauce, and, without hesitating, put it in her mouth. It was a wonderful sight. While all the diners around me were scooping the terrible things from their plates and stuffing them into their ever-open mouths as they carried on talking—as if eating were something impersonal; a mere matter of taking on nutrition—she paid the same attention to her salad as someone who has grown and picked it themselves. She was, however, not only eating but also glancing now and then at an electronic device lying neatly alongside her knife. From time to time, it caught her attention—though her gestures gave one to understand that it was nothing of importance—and she would shake her head so that her dark hair, tied up in a ponytail, bobbed about for a second. She had a delicate Madonna-like face, a radiant face with shining eyes over which anyone watching her could see a shadow pass. How beautiful it looked, this split-second shift in which the perfectly composed upper part of her face transformed itself into a disturbing abyss. In that moment, I would have given my life to know who had dared to disturb that face while she was eating.

When she began to look round for the waitress, I got in first and asked the waitress to pass on my request to the young woman eating salad, that I might ask her a question about Trakl; after this half hour of spying on her, hopefully unnoticed, it was clear to me that she was the only person at this late hour in this restaurant who would know where the poet was buried.

When the waitress shouted the message from the silent diner across the room into the woman's ear, I saw how her concentration lapsed for a second and how she looked over in my direction. A flash of warmth went through me. I felt, in that very moment, all the troubles of the world melt away, along with all its misery. I jumped up much too quickly, grabbed a napkin from the buffet and rushed over to the woman who looked at me without anger, more mockingly. I wondered, she said, why you had been staring at me in that strange way but I'd never have guessed you wanted to ask me about Trakl. I usually have to turn away very different sorts of questions.

I was too ashamed to reply and couldn't think of anything that would justify my presence at her side. I was much older, a little scruffy, and at the moment I had nothing I could throw into the scales on my behalf. I just want to spend a few moments in your company, I shouted, too loud and too hysterical to sound convincing. But I didn't need to explain anything. She knew everything, saw everything at a glance, and maybe even felt a little sorry for me as I crouched beside her with my napkin and asked her to show me the way to Trakl's grave, when what I really wanted, and what she had long recognized, was to find the true path to her heart.

I carefully folded the napkin with her directions and put it in my jacket pocket, next to my heart. As I thanked her, I felt tears well up in my eyes, more unstoppable and liberating than I had experienced for years. Oh good heavens, the young woman said dryly, that has been building up for some time, has it not? You will have to let that all out before you walk to Trakl's grave. She laid her hand on my arm and allowed me to blubber while she fetched more napkins for me to cry into and ruffled my hair as a series of sighs threatened to convulse me: she was, in all, a presence in whose protection I felt safe and free from fear. And, if I may say so, she also kept the other guests at bay who had gathered round our table, either out of curiosity or concern, and were transfixed by the pieta taking place before their eyes.

With this beautiful woman I walked through the uplands of Peru and through Central Park; she dragged me from my sickbed in Africa and held out a walking stick across the roaring waters of the Amazon so that I could find my way back to the bank. We ate dumplings at Hradčany Castle in Prague and salted cod in a harbour restaurant in Portugal; on each occasion I said that there must be some mistake, I'm not the person you think I am, and she looked at me so kindly with her wise eyes that I would have taken on any identity just to remain in her presence.

When I awoke, the waitress was sitting next to me cashing up for the night. I looked at her torn fingernails and her splintered nail polish. She had put a rubber band around the large notes and was just about to count the coins which she had stacked into towers of ten each. The owner (or the head waiter?) was sitting a few tables away with a beer, and next to him the last guest was loitering with a dog whose nose looked as though it had been squashed by a kick. Apart from the clicking of the coins there was silence. The boyfriend of the woman sitting next to you came to pick her up, the waitress said, without interrupting her counting. She says hello and that under no circumstances should you go to the cemetery tonight.

I paid, gave the waitress a tip and made my way to the Grey Bear that, in the starlit night, I found within a few minutes. I had left the window open and it was ice cold in the room. I kicked off my drenched shoes, got into bed fully clothed, turned off the light and fell quickly into a dreamless sleep, the image of the nameless woman still before my eyes.

The next morning, I set off straight away. I no longer wanted to go to Trakl's grave but to Reschen Pass. In the night, some kind of switch had been thrown in my mind. At the top of the pass it looked as though a violent storm had blown away all the trees, leaving only a few stalks, like tatty microphones, poking out of the grass laid flat by the rain. It was a moonscape and, in fact, just as I thought this, I saw a pale moon high above the pass, impervious even to the winds. A laughable moon, I thought, an evil, cold star. But at least it knows where it belongs and shines its last waning light on the wonders stretched out below, before it becomes a victim of the rain.

Although I didn't have a map, I was able to find the village and the hotel I was searching for straight away. The village lay on a hill and the hotel was to the side and slightly to the south. From its windows the view was down to Adige Valley; above, the huge mountains towered to form an impressive pass. Now, in late autumn, when the trees have lost their leaves and only the pine trees and larches provide any sign of life under the glowering skies, one can contemplate that which is unimaginable between the apple blossom in spring and the early days of November: that there is a certain type of person living here, who, out of some abyssal despair, is capable of the most brutal acts. How often, in the last but one decade of the last century, I had heard stories from a little village in the province of Bolzano about the brutality with which disputes between neighbours had been settled. How often, after having been away for a short while, I had met friends who were missing an eye or had lost all reason after some fight. Even today I think of one of my neighbour's sons, who, because of some ridiculous test of strength, drove his souped-up moped into a ravine. All they found of him was a bag of bones. The wolf-like character of these people, combined with a naive Catholicism, has had a terrible effect on the culture of these valleys, especially during winter, and it can barely be disguised by the apple blossom of summer. The house I'd bought because I needed a roof over my head in a place that was glad to see me and to which I longed to return had been sold; I didn't want to live among these strange misfits who became so brutalized in winter that they called down plague and ruin on one another. When my neighbour stripped his dead sheepdog's fur from its body and made himself a fur collar, I had had enough—I never wanted to return.

But now the place had drawn me back again.

My father, a classical archaeologist, hanged himself in Rome when his students, whom he was fond of, dug with diligence and a certain schadenfreude into his Nazi files and published accounts of his activities. In his last years, he had withdrawn to a Benedictine abbey in Farfa in the Sabine hills outside Rome, in order to study its Gothic murals which he had written about, years before, in his doctoral dissertation. He made the mistake in many of his publications of writing about Catholic Germans living outside Germany, whom he saw as having reached their pinnacle in Farfa, in such an exaggeratedly admiring way that many of his closest students began to ask themselves what the author who had heaped such solemn praise on the double-headed eagle of the Holy Roman Empire of the German Nation had got up to during the Nazi period. Stylistic idiosyncrasies and old-fashioned formulations brought him down. The results of the research were devastating: intrigues, denunciation, firings because of anti-German attitudes, the documents all clearly carried his signature, and, even if it was not evident whether he had just signed them because he was in charge, he saw no other way out than suicide. Of course we didn't want to believe that someone captivated by Gothic art and au fait with every other Italian picture could be responsible for such terrible things, but the proof was incontrovertible. Did he get into this terrible situation because he wanted to get on or did he sincerely believe that foreign German culture, as he called it, could be united with that of a fascist Germany? In the end, he was obviously too weak to invent a different past for himself unlike his colleagues in art history. For many years, I imagined him sitting in his little Roman flat and deciding to kill himself.

I had driven to Rome with my mother in order to collect my father's possessions from his little two-room flat in Via Nomentana and bring them home, and to carry out any necessary formalities. It was a catastrophic journey. For the first time in my life, I was confined with my mother for two long days, trapped with a woman screaming at God and the world and cursing both families, my father's and her own. My little store of illusions was soon used up, dissolved by my her hatred. But I can't say whether it was disappointed love that led her to such fury or whether her own life had become pointless. She had transformed into an impervious lump of hatred: questions and arguments, no matter how carefully put, were simply deflected off her.

We had stopped at the hotel—the one to which I have now returned—in order to rest before driving on to Rome. She forced me to take Room No. 2 with her, a small room in which stood, as they did today, two narrow beds, a rustic painted wardrobe and an enamel washbasin, at which my mother, whom I had never before seen undressed, bent over in order to wash her armpits with a flannel. There was no chance of getting any sleep that night: she gave off a ceaseless volley of oaths and turned over and over in her bed so that I worried that she would wake the hotel owners sleeping in the next room. The next morning they did indeed seem happy to see the back of us. They had never had to accommodate such an angry person before.

My mother insisted we stop here again, on the way back. My father's papers, notes, letters and manuscripts had been stuffed into a bag. His books, together with library books about the Benedictines of Farfa, were collected by a librarian from the Hertziana. The rest—a few vases, cutlery, an old TV, a collection of postcards, Etruscan trinkets, a worn-out carpet and his clothes—I gave to the caretaker who, as a result, spoke of my father in the most exaggerated tones as a generous, friendly tenant, and how it was merely jealousy and resentment that had driven him to his death. I pictured for myself how the caretaker would visit the flea market the next weekend in order to sell my father's belongings, and how a short time later a Somalian or a Syrian would be walking through Rome in my father's double-breasted jacket, his umbrella in hand and on his feet his worn-out shoes. By the evening, the flat was empty. Apart from a few secrets, my father had left nothing behind, at least nothing of any great significance. When I stood with the caretaker at the front door of the little house in Porta Pia, I removed, as the last thing, a picture of me that had been pinned to the wall above the telephone, and on which was written my telephone number in purple felt pen. Even back then, on the unhappiest day of my life, I couldn't remember having spoken to him on the telephone from Rome. I visited him a few times and we looked at a few churches but, if I remember correctly, he seemed to me to be a particularly well-informed tour guide rather than a father.

And so my mother and I drove back north. Despite her desolate condition, she had dealt with all the official arrangements. Father was to be buried—God knows why—in Germany, even though he had expressly asked for a grave in Farfa. Once again, I had to listen to her rage against him and his blasted family who had conspired to force her into an 'early' grave. On the way back, I insisted that I should have my own room, not least because I feared I might hit her in order to bring her back to her senses. I had hardly locked my door after the evening meal than she started hammering on it with both fists and screeching through her tears so that everyone could hear: if you think that you are your father's son, then you have made a big mistake. But how was I to believe a woman so distraught? And what would it have changed anyway?

I never saw my mother again. That night, I called my sisters in Regensburg and told them to pick her up. Shortly after midnight, I drove home alone and piled up my father's papers in the spare room, where they are stored to this very day. There is supposed to be an answer at the end of life, but there is none. It is a petty-bourgeois conceit that things should come to a proper conclusion, a cowardly refusal to recognize the power of coincidence. The bad thing was, of course, that after my father's violent death I had also lost my mother. I remembered only her rage-filled expression, a mask of hatred that this gentle woman had stuck over her own face.

Now, for the third time, I was staying in this little village hotel. The owners, now ancient, recognized me immediately and allowed me to sleep in Room No. 2. I stayed for three days. I lost all sense of time, and the idea that time could soon run out did not irritate me in any way. It had run out.

By day I went for long walks; in the evenings I sat by the fire with the hotel owners, stroking the cat on my lap. I called it Ezra, in memory of an American poet I'd visited in my youth in nearby

Brunnenburg. It was a visit without words to an old man with a straw hat on his head who allowed me to stammer a few words of appreciation without even looking at me. God knows what he thought. Maybe he didn't even know I was there. The cat was missing its left eye and half its right ear. On the other hand, it purred loud enough for three.

Soon after I arrived, the owners had given me my father's notebook which I had left behind unread. Bound in artificial brown leather, it was filled to the last page with his tiny handwriting. Even the last page inside the back cover was covered in notes. They were from the year of my birth.

On the last evening, after a wonderful meal and a bottle of wine, I sat again with Ezra in front of the roaring fireplace, fetched my manuscript from my bag and threw it, with my father's notebook, into the fire. The cover held out against the flames for a short while, then gave up.

It was high time I started a new book.

A WRITER'S LIFE

On my seventieth birthday, I received a friendly letter from an antiquarian book dealer in Stuttgart asking whether, when I died, I would like him to come and take away my library. Collection in place of payment, the argument went: books were not worth more than that. As long as one continued reading them or kept them about as the repository of one's reading life they had a certain meaning, but then, after their owner's departure, they were evidently as lifeless and worthless as the stones, feathers and postcards that collected on the shelves in front of them. There were at least 15,000 volumes in my house, in a village close to Ravensburg, organized according to a system that only I knew. Rare first editions stood next to books I had found by chance, books signed by colleagues next to novels that had sometimes not even been unpacked and which had been sent to me with a request for attention. If the back cover was emblazoned with the words 'I haven't read anything like this for a long time!' then it would not be me that freed it from its cellophane. My rare complete edition of Max Scheler stood next to my little Novalis collection which, in turn, shared a shelf with esoteric travel literature. Only I knew what could be found where. Some of the rare items, such as the first edition of *Ulysses*, were hidden behind others because some of my friends had the habit of taking advantage of the apparent chaos to help themselves. Occasionally, I would come across my books in dealers' catalogues: like my signed edition of Scheerbart or the copy of Paul Valéry's essays that he had dedicated to Léautaud. Even the lovely collection of postcards sent by Rolf Dieter Brinkmann from Rome, where he updated me about his reading of Brentano had, over the course of years, found new owners. Sometimes I toyed with the idea of . . . No, that doesn't belong here.

I was sitting in the train home from Hamburg, and had a bad headache. The previous evening, my publisher had thrown a big party to mark the publication of his spring catalogue. A good deal was drunk, as in the old days. I still knew some of the older literary critics and we talked about the old days, as usual, and in glowing terms, as usual. I don't know why I agreed to such a stressful journey—in the end, some internal voice had convinced me. In the afternoon, I walked to the Kunsthalle so I could bid farewell to some of the pictures, because it suddenly dawned on me that I would probably never return to Hamburg. I was almost the only visitor and was able to wander with Ruisdael's walkers over the dunes and look at the washerwomen without being at all disturbed. The gnarled willows in the pictures were supposed to be interpreted as Christian symbols but I regarded them with pleasure as willows, just like the willow trees of my childhood. My publisher met me in the cafe at the Kunsthalle so that we could go on to the 'Culture Factory' where the party was to take place. Where workers once used to toil, there were now cultural events. An improvement, at least. There were no workers to be seen at the party—they obviously stayed clear of their old workplace. Brain-workers, one or two of my former colleagues used to call themselves, so as to reduce the distance between them and real workers, but the distance remained considerable.

On the way to the party, my publisher—a man of many talents, the foremost of which was to fire up his authors with inspiration—sketched out the plan for the new book I should write. I loved him for his almost childlike fondness for literature which he perceived as constantly under threat more than anything from the literary scene which was deteriorating every day, and of which, of course, he was a prominent part. He particularly had it in for young authors who demanded huge advances but could not write. Some of them, he shouted into the wind, were so blonde that nothing could be expected of them in future either. I had to laugh, as he only worked himself up like this in order to praise me indirectly; since I had never demanded an advance and because I knew full well that, at his party, he would do all that he could to get close to the young blonde authors, and he knew it too. The more harmless they are, the better they are for business. In order to accommodate the multitude of young authors, he had created several dedicated series and imprints where they could publish but which, he emphasized, would not 'interfere'—one of his favourite phrases—with the parts of the business where the serious literature took place. The pure should not be 'interfered with' by the impure in any way. That was his main worry. I was part of the pure, he was at pains to say.

His plan, which he laid out to me as we walked along the windy banks of the Alster, was that I should write a new version of a novel I had published forty years earlier. It had been my greatest success; the radio piece developed out of the novel was aired regularly; for many years, schoolchildren were obliged to interpret it in their lessons; and, eventually, there was a not particularly good, but very successful, film version that was even shown abroad. That book earned me a tidy sum. It told the story of a patriarch, one of the economic founding fathers of West Germany, like Grundig or Schickedanz, a pompous figure whose only ambition was to line his pockets, but who then found himself cast as a socially significant figure, something that went on to become more important to him than the money. That man was now on his deathbed, with his five children gathered around him. Quite remarkably, I had given him only sons. He asked these five men in the prime of life what they intended to do with the company and the money they would inherit: their answers would determine how he would write his last will and testament. When that was done, he wanted to die. The book was written in a strangely formal style. Sometimes it sounded archaic and sometimes like a fairy tale. In any case, readers back then loved it because they could all identify with one of the sons. I had spent a lot of time thinking about how to write the Magnificent Five so that they would truly represent all possible variants: there was the thrifty one and the wasteful one; the risk-taker and the risk-averse; the one who always had the common good in mind; the one who wished to flatter his father; and the hard-nosed expansionist who always had his eye on the world market. In the end (which today I would have to say was rather flat), the father suffers a heart attack and dies just after speaking to the youngest son who has outlined his social vision for the future of the firm. In the last chapter is a short description of how the five sons, regardless of the highly ethical assurances they have just made, fall upon one another and push the firm to the brink of bankruptcy.

I had not picked up the book in the intervening years but, if I remember right, it was his intention—at least that's what the critics thought at the time—to decide in favour of a socially responsible business model. Was I really such a megalomaniac? No, quite the opposite. Back then, I was interested in how this particular generation viewed itself—the one that had been through the war and the 'reconstruction' and was now about to leave the stage—and how it was viewed by its sons. How did Nazis become good citizens? I was also interested in how, out of the blue, money, capital, had become the only thing that mattered.

The idea my publisher was trying to outline in the teeth of the increasingly unpleasant wind, not unusual in this city, was that I should write a contemporary version, mapped onto the development of capitalism since then; and for this he was prepared to offer me, quite against his usual habits, a horrendous advance. He worked himself up into a frenzy, despite the inclement weather, and mentioned every family business from Bertelsmann to

Quant, Otto and Neckermann, so that I was poised to ask whether he might actually be the man to write this, when he came to his concluding argument for the urgency of this new version: namely, women. You have to include women, he shouted, red-faced. The women in the first row and, of course, the women in the second who spend the money that is made in the first row, that army of female art collectors and directors of foundations who helped create Germany's image in the world and give capitalism a new face. The women at the patriarch's bed, he screamed, who have just come back from Bayreuth or the Biennale in Venice, and who complain about the minimum wage, dressed up to the nines in their wickedly expensive clothes, but who offer the workers in Pakistan only pennies; and who talk at the old man's deathbed about whether the health insurance will pay up for his care. Because I didn't say a word, he interjected after each of these propositions: do you know what I mean? Praise be to God, we arrived at the party and he finally shut up. Think about it, he called out to me before delivering himself into the arms of the blonde authors.

At the party, I was introduced to my new editor. The old one had unfortunately retired. I had worked with her for forty years: a conscientious woman who tended towards dry irony. She would eradicate every misplaced comma in my manuscript and explain, in the margin, why I should do without it but would also always insert a comma somewhere else so that it was not altogether lost. She was not only an expert on the German spelling reform but also on my opening sentences, which we often worked on, over a period of weeks, by correspondence. In my farewell letter, I had asked whether, should I ever write another book, she would be prepared to act as my editor on a freelance basis, but she had declined. Apparently she had been very badly treated, or at least she no longer wanted to have anything to do with the publisher. She was now growing roses not far from Freiburg.

The new editor, Dagmar, pulled me into a corner of the cold festival hall as soon as we met so as to tell me the plan for my new novel; obviously, they had already been talking about it and had assumed that I would say yes. Unusually for a fiction editor, she had studied sociology, which made her interest in this project more understandable. She spoke very quickly, pretty much without full stops and commas, and kneaded every sentence with her firm restless hands. As I had not given a moment's thought to this new edition, I just let her talk and contented myself with watching her, drinking the terrible red wine and keeping quiet. Truth be told, I had decided not to write anything ever again, and by no means a novel. I wanted to look through my notebooks, publish excerpts, perhaps put together an annotated volume, or maybe an essay. It was for others to write novels now. There were enough young writers waiting to be discovered and promoted. And all of them wanted to talk to her and were advancing dangerously, but were kept at a distance, something I found flattering. She only wanted to talk to me.

If I understood her aright, she imagined that I would not only describe the changes in 'entrepreneurial culture' but also create a portrait of capitalism after the banking crisis as a form of literary, and therefore comprehensible, one-stop critique of capitalist economics. We need something like that, she said, and if anyone is able to outline the new configurations and constellations and how they impact the individual and society in general, then it's you. You will be writing the first genuine book of the twenty-first century. It will knock all other attempts to describe the fundamental workings of capitalism into a cocked hat.

Dagmar talked and talked in the way that her generation has learnt to do—recognize the problem, offer an immediate solution, then straight down to work—and I got more tired and ever-more convinced that she was talking to the wrong person. At the lowest point of my exhaustion—I was very close to disappearing under the table—this beautiful woman suddenly stood up, embraced me and thanked me in the most exaggerated terms for agreeing to do the book. We'll work it out somehow, don't worry. She would accompany me every step of the way, she whispered, which sounded very much like surveillance to me, and if needs be, she would come and visit me for lengthy periods of time so as to be on the spot and support my progress with word and deed. It will be a great book, she called back to me as she was leaving, whereas I was now quite sure that I would under no circumstances write the book, not this one and nor any other.

With this resolution in mind, I stood up and was immediately swept up into the maelstrom. An old writer lost among crowds of young people who were a little jealous of him because he had had the much-desired ear of Dagmar. In the meantime, it had become so noisy that no one could hear themselves speak. It's amazing how loud book people can become if you give them free alcohol. They sit for the whole day quiet as a mouse in front of their sheets of white paper, which fill only slowly, but after the first glass of wine they think they know it all. A critic, whom I used to pity because he had to review a book every week and had absolutely nothing to say, had even climbed onto a table to demonstrate something or other. Whatever it was, was unintelligible, but everyone was screaming with laughter. On my way out, I wondered what a party for marine biologists or experts on prime numbers would look like.

The next morning, I was picked up outside Hotel Wedina in a pre-ordered taxi that ferried me and my little travel bag the 500 metres to the main station. The express train was waiting. With fresh newspapers and a Simenon book from the station bookshop that I hoped I hadn't already read under a different title, I looked for and found my compartment and my reserved seat.

And there, sitting opposite me, was Dagmar, my new editor.

2

My little trip to Hamburg stayed with me for a long time. I thought of my late friend Peter Rühmkorf, with whom I had undertaken some of the craziest journeys of my life. We did a reading together in the Goethe Institute in Istanbul at the time of the military junta, where, as we read, young Anatolian soldiers with machine guns came and stood behind us, causing Rühmkorf to stutter and break out in a cold sweat. We had been informed the night before that two harmless tourists who had not responded when hailed by a soldier had been gunned down. What do we do if they don't understand us? Rühmkorf asked me, while I was more afraid that the young lads would smell what sort of drugs he had mixed with his tobacco. Whatever happens, they'll shoot us, I had whispered back, and it will be our last appearance. He was the most pleasant hypochondriac imaginable. As a matter of principle he took the twelve pills he had to swallow every day with a little brandy, which meant that the bottle was always empty. Because there was a night-time curfew, we had to go to the jazz club in the afternoon where, of course, he fell in love with the barmaid, which meant that we had to spend the night on the hard benches in the bar, wrapped only in the fog emanating from his pre-rolled cigarettes. I was reminded of our wonderful journey into the Australian outback where he greeted the linguistically gifted corvids, who waited solemnly and on their best behaviour outside our window every morning, with Maoist slogans. Much to the amazement of the kangaroos and koalas, the birds were able to repeat these slogans after about a week. Rühmkorf and many more of my Hamburg friends were now long dead, so why should I go to Hamburg again?

I have never been what one might call a conventional writer. After wasting my time at university, I spent many years in development aid and wrote three books about hopelessness in Africa, which, as far as facts are concerned, are of course now completely outdated, but which are occasionally cited, guaranteeing them a long lifespan in paperback. I became an 'Africa expert', much in demand, and, because everyone back then was interested in Mao's China or Castro's Cuba, but not Africa, I could say whatever came into my head. But I always told the truth.

After that, I wrote a series of short novels of which *The Patriarch* was the most successful but which, apart from the money, also brought me the envy of a number of proper writers who could only dream of my sales. Moderating a talk show put an end to my reputation in the world of literature until I published my first book of poetry, which then made me into an outsider in the business, a role that I play well and happily.

I had given up on the whole writing business apart from a few radio plays and the occasional essay and, of course, my unpublished daily notes which ran to several thousand pages. My ambition to take up the reins again and to work towards a publication of these volumes was limited. What would it bring? Who should, indeed who would want to, read it? My loyal publisher's repeated suggestions that I hand over the volumes to a young literary scholar for evaluation I disregarded, when said young scholar, after flicking through one of the volumes, came to the view that no one of his generation would be interested in a description of the syncretic religions of Africa. When I dropped the name Hubert Fichte into the conversation, with whom I had often discussed my experiences and who had always encouraged me to turn them into a book, the young man confessed that he had never heard of him, so I decided to let the whole business lie. I did not wish to entrust my insights to this generation of smart alecs, who know everything and nothing. I took up contact with a literary archive, which was happy to take on my note-books, and, because I promised to add some of my correspondence to the bundle—not least a brief exchange with Nelson Mandela—they promised to transcribe all of them after my death and make them available for research purposes. Whether they would stick to those promises was, to be frank, of little interest to me. The vanity of thinking about my posthumous reputation was completely lost on me. I was far too attached to life to be concerned with such laughable trivialities.

My favourite thing was to listen to music. It was, for me, the only possibility of achieving a concentration of spirit. As I had no immediate neighbours, I could turn the volume up as loud as I wanted and, in the summer, lie in a reclining chair and allow the music to banish any thought of productive work. The inner agitation that came over me when I listened to the Diabelli Variations raised me above any ambition to write another book or to extend the 72 cm that my books took up on the shelf by a further 2. If at all, then I wanted to write about clouds, about the sky and

the pure crystal air, about the smouldering fire that
is idleness and the oblivious gazing that drives
away all disappointment. I wanted to take care
of the garden too, that had got into a terrible state.
When I moved into the house several years ago, I
had gone around it with abandon: scattering
handfuls of flower seeds on the lawn and planting
my favourite berries along the fence; raspberries
and gooseberries, along with lilac and hazel, but I
had not taken care of them since. I had no time. I
wrote and wanted to become famous for writing.
I travelled so as to distract myself from writing.
Now I didn't want to do anything. Just read, listen
to music and tend the overgrown garden that I
wanted to leave in a good state when I went. But,
strangely, I didn't even have the energy to manage
that. My only ambition was to arrive at myself.

3

Clever Dagmar moved into the summerhouse. She
should come and go as she pleased, I told her. That
small building was the place I stored my old magazines: Max Bense's *rot*; *Monat*, where I first read
the poems of Wallace Stevens; *Merkur*; *Texte und
Zeichen*; the *Neue Rundschau*; a complete run of
the journals *Brenner* and *Fackel*; the editions of
Hyperion edited by Franz Blei and Carl Sternheim,
containing contributions by Kafka; *manuskripte*
and the *Frankfurter Hefte*, *Sinn und Form* and

many others, including all the additions of the *Nouvelle Revue Française* of which I was particularly proud, although the lot of it would be seen merely as recycling these days. At least Dagmar would have all the reading she needed for the rest of her life. Dagmar had no intention, however, of poking around in the old journals but asked for permission to read my notebooks in order, as she put it, to get inside my thinking. My thinking! Good heavens! But I allowed her to do so. As far as I was concerned, she could read herself rotten on my old scribblings. Her constitution, by the way, was more than robust. Not only did this sturdy woman—from a farming family in Schleswig Holstein and a master of the art of milking cows— eat all the fatty sausages that she brought with her and which, as far as I knew, were only liked, and indeed eaten, in her home state, she also soon became a much-loved customer at the restaurant in the nearby village, where she consumed, in very short order, their entire repertoire of German ravioli and spätzle. When I looked out of the window of my study across to her window, something I did more or less constantly at the beginning, I often saw her in a little vest, doing physical exercises, as if she wanted to prove to me that she was not limited to carrying out the exercises of an editor.

I never really got the measure of her. Sometimes she indulged her tendency towards indiscretion and gossiped endlessly about the unpleasant quirks of my publisher, her boss; at other times, she clammed up when I enquired about the antics of some of the writers she was responsible for. One could feel the melancholy behind every offensive sentence and the abyss behind her silence. As far as conventional morality was concerned, she was agnostic, which I rather liked. When I once asked how her love life was doing, she said gruffly that that was bugger all to do with me; but a day later she regaled me with repulsive details about her affair, as she called it, with an actor from the Thalia Theatre to whom, despite his cheating on her many times, she was not able to give his marching orders. And so he stands, she said, like an empty barrel in the corner, until I roll him back into bed.

She came and went as she pleased. At first she was there for a week in order to settle in, then later she came at weekends and stayed on for the Monday. Then what she called a bridge day which would allow her to live in the summerhouse for half a week, until the summer when, finally, she spent her holidays with me without the actor putting in so much as a single appearance. So that I formed the impression that she lived with me full time and only occasionally went to Hamburg for work. Of course I avoided asking her about the legitimacy of her peripatetic work habits which stood in stark contrast to the strict discipline I had come to know from the publisher; and when I once plucked up the courage to broach the topic in the vaguest of terms, she said that she was always working since she always had manuscripts with her. In the summer holidays, we drove her red VW Golf down to Lake Constance to go swimming and made short trips to the local area; and when I fell into bed, dead tired of an evening, I could see the light burning in her window and devoutly hoped that she was working and would carry on working until late into the night.

Myself, I was not working on the book as expected. During the summer, I had written an essay for a *festschrift* about the Viennese poet H. C. Artmann, whom I had got to know in Berlin in the previous century: an agonizing birth of twenty pages. The older one becomes, the more often one is invited to contribute to this kind of volume, burdensome commissions that are badly paid and never reach an audience. If they do, it is in all likelihood an emeritus German professor from Oklahoma who doubts whether a certain metaphor used by Artmann was really coined by him or whether perhaps it had not appeared in Polger before that, about whom he is enclosing an offprint of an article from *German Literature Today* in the hope of getting to the bottom of the matter. Because, naturally, the metaphor does not even appear in the article, one is obliged to write back and say one has looked for it but is sadly none the wiser, which leads to further correspondence until one or other of the correspondents, willingly or unwillingly, departs this life. Since I still write my letters by hand, thank God, and entrust them to the post, it can take up to three weeks before I get a letter back, which increases the chances that I might at any moment have the final letter in my hand.

Dagmar, of course, assumed, when she interrupted me at lunch, that I was working on the bloody book and I did nothing to dissuade her of that, although this cowardly attitude struck me as pitiful, not least because she believed ever-more strongly in it. She deluged me with articles and books about the general state of the economy, lectured me with tales of evil tax-dodgers who had been discovered salting their money away in Switzerland or on some English island, and fed me titbits about the life and death of big corporate bosses. She was of the opinion that a certain Herr Zumwinkel should play a role in my book. To her mind, he was made for it: all show and no substance, she said, a philistine through and through and in the middle was the money that this person, who played a certain role at the top of the post office, was able to siphon directly into his bank account avoiding the tax man altogether. But what did a greedy postman who couldn't seem to get enough have to do with my philosophical thoughts? Nothing. This terrible kind of specimen, who were given the opportunity by the economic miracle to make themselves rich at the cost of society, were so beneath my contempt that I was unable to fit them into any of my categories. The Federal Republic of Germany was stuffed full of such creatures, and any announcement that a Swiss bank was to be forced to open its accounts resulted in dentists, art dealers and spare-parts traders with dodgy pockets contacting the tax authorities in order to declare the millions that had slipped their minds. I would prefer somebody like the manager Thomas Middelhoff, a driven man who probably really did believe that he could steal a march on capital. I could imagine his ironic sausage-dog face at the patriarch's deathbed, explaining to the old man, in his reinforced sheets, that he had to do what he did, that the conditions in advanced capitalism had left him no choice but to cut a few corners. He could have played his part in my book, a vain, comical episode, as a dodgy rogue alongside the other rogues making up the beggars' chorus. We just wanted to make a bit of cash, and, because everyone turned a blind eye, we put the cash in our accounts without a thought. But why should I dedicate a whole book to this gang? Why should this unpatriotic crew of crooks keep me from writing an essay or poem about a spectacular sunset?

But I was unable to come clean with Dagmar. When she sent me painstakingly footnoted excerpts from the business sections of various newspapers while she was away, at a book fair or a business meeting, I noticed how much I missed her. As long as she was around, I felt a certain capacity to work, even if not on the much-anticipated book. When she had been gone for a while, I fell back to reading, listening to music and dreaming. Within three weeks, I lost myself completely and became a strange solitary figure who conducted deep conversations with Schopenhauer or succumbed to Leopardi's bottomless pessimism, entirely unable to muster any patience for the problems of modern capitalism, let alone for the women caught up in this grubby game of money. The deep chasm between my state of mind and the one I was obliged to present soon became abundantly clear to me, and I knew I had to tell Dagmar, so as to save face. If she were to come and 'look in' at Christmas, as she wrote—thank God she hated the telephone as much as I did—I would be forced to tell her the whole truth.

4

At Christmas I listened out for the sound of her VW outside, but in vain. She had probably dragged her fat actor into bed and wouldn't let him go. I caught myself checking the programme of the Thalia Theatre on the Internet to find out if he was appearing. He wasn't. His only appearance was on

23rd December, when he was to read Dickens in the afternoon, and then nothing until 3rd January. Dagmar had time, therefore, to come and visit me, and she could certainly have sent me a message with the lie that her father in Heide/Holstein had been taken sick or that her grandmother had died, but there was nothing. Not a word. Of course I tried to convince myself that I had been lucky, that I had managed to duck an unwelcome bullet, but it didn't work. I felt anxiety rising within me, which took away my pleasure in doing nothing. I realized that there was no one who would relieve me of the burden of my own responsibility. I was truly alone. In order to calm myself down, I read Tolstoy's short story 'How Much Land Does a Man Need?' a story for which I, in order to avoid finishing my own book, could provide a long afterword. On these thirty pages was collected everything that I needed to say about the theory of needs, only put in a simpler, clearer, more convincing way. I had always been mistrustful of the verbosity of theory. The eternal repetition of a hundred citations that were supposed to put the world in context, even if they weren't able to explain it. What were the thick tomes I read in my youth against one good poem? Why did I not write a canto about money, like Ezra Pound did about the abolition of money by Silvio Gesell, even if neither money nor envy had been abolished. Or maybe a song about the cowrie shell? Or . . .

So I wrote a Christmas letter to Dagmar, admitted how much I was missing her and how much I hoped we would meet again, although I also said at the end that I hoped she had finally found her place in the arms of her actor, etc. The letter was a hopeless evasive mess with only one true message: come back, you are needed here.

Sometimes I went into the summerhouse at night and sat at her desk where she had left her writing pads and yellow Post-its and the biros taken from the hotels she had stayed in. The wardrobe was full of her summer dresses and bathing suits and in the bottom her sandals and baskets and all the bits and pieces she had brought from Hamburg each week. On the bookshelves, in front of my journals, were her incomprehensible books on economic history and economic statistics, on German entrepreneurs and economic criminality and among them the ones that I had recommended she read, from Leopardi to the poems of Nicholas Born and the novels of Hermann Lenz. I had lent her so many books so as to displace the various contemporary novels she had brought with her to stimulate my imagination, or, to make it even better, as she had said. I had made a start on some of them, usually up to the point where the first love affair was described, and then shut them immediately. I felt a strong reluctance rise up inside me, a bottomless sadness that was stronger than the curiosity about their sham effects that otherwise overcomes me automatically when I read my fellow writers' novels. Often I read them only with an eye for technique, how they were constructed, what tricks were used in order to stand out from the crowd, but the content was mostly of no interest to me. Of course that is only partly true, because in the moment I have this thought, all the contemporary novels appear before me that I have read with great respect. I am probably just allergic to originality. Original authors are highly suspect, as far as I am concerned, and if they also try to give the impression of obscurity, as Dagmar put it 'the shop is closed for business'. I noticed that that I had started looking for excuses not to have to write any more. I had probably become a reactionary. To be a writer who didn't write seemed to me to be the one true goal of a writing life.

I sat silently at 'her' desk and prayed for her, which was probably the most extreme sign of despair. If things were bad for her then my prayers would not help, and if things were going well, she would think of it as an imposition. I, on the other hand, as became clearer to me, felt better and enjoyed a brighter mood every time I sat and meditated at her little desk. So in that sense everything was all right.

At one such moment, I absentmindedly opened an exercise book that was sticking out from a pile of papers. I really only wanted to look at her handwriting, I reassured myself, but naturally I knew I was doing something forbidden. Although it was the middle of the night, I stood up to draw the curtains and lock the door. There, in her handwriting, I discovered me. She had obviously copied out those parts that she thought were important from the notebooks I had in all innocence given her to 'get to know me'. Not everything of mine that I read was repulsive or bad; but by leaving out what was apparently irrelevant—or at least what Dagmar thought irrelevant—the impression was created of a true aphorist, one who produced only weighty thoughts and ignored the small everyday things of life, which, of course, are in fact the staple concern of my journals. It suddenly seemed to me that Dagmar had cut me into two, torn me in two. On the one hand, an endlessly rationalizing, somewhat pedantic, thinker who needed to be saved, and, on the other, a citizen of a somehow-functioning republic who had said yes to life and could therefore be forgotten without further ado. Now here was the thinker, sitting at the table and reading the brooding cogitations of a lonely wanderer, until the despair of it all tightened my throat. For sure, I had written every line I read in Dagmar's notes; but this was not a manuscript written by me, but by a synthetic and not particularly likeable author who had the darkest thoughts about the state of the world. I read an author who aspired to be similar to me but, as much as he tried, just wasn't able to. What a notion of hers, to want to create a different person to the one who had taken her in and looked after her in such a friendly way, not to speak of the other things. Bold as brass. I had invited the devil into my house.

I left the book open on the table as if it was nothing to do with me. If it had been my publisher's intention to suck my lifeblood from me, then he had been sorely mistaken. If it had been Dagmar's idea to manipulate me for her own purposes, then I would not be able to invite her back. Good riddance to her; I hope she is happy with her actor. The question that tortured me until dawn—and I was amazed at what resources of self-torture I had buried within—was, however: how many journals had she already filled with my desolate thoughts? The whole summer long she had been blithely taking my notebooks over to the summerhouse to get a better look, as she put it, at my darker side. Sometimes, at breakfast the next day, she would remind me of certain entries that I had long forgotten. Sometimes she spoke to me like a child, chastising me for having such dark thoughts: at my age, it could only lead to bitterness, she said. Sometimes, if not very often, she would praise me when my entries seemed to her to have been particularly apt. Of course, I also remembered that she had several times said we should do something with these notebooks, that they were too interesting to be left to just moulder. Yes, she actually used the word moulder. The stab of pain it caused I remember quite well. So you think I'm as good as dead already, I asked her, and she answered, as quick as a flash, with her Holstinian dry wit, that it was possible to moulder while still alive—I should just look around.

The Christmas period would have been spent in bitterness if I hadn't bumped into someone at Christmas Mass in the neighbouring village, who, when I told him that I was spending Christmas alone, invited me to join him to eat the seasonal goose. We stood next to each other and he sang carols with great gusto and was so miserably out of tune that sometimes, much to his confusion, I laughed out loud. He was so out of tune that he didn't even notice how the notes shot off in different directions from his open mouth. Between carols I had time to look around the church and was shocked to see, in the face of an angel bringing glad tidings as he climbed lustily towards the rood loft, the features of none other than Dagmar: her beautiful, broad, sturdy face, the cheerful mask behind which she hid her devilish intentions, beamed down at me. I had to avert my gaze and fix it instead on our suffering Lord who has been hanging, unmoving, on the cross for two thousand years now. He, with his broken eyes, wanted to speak through us because he could not speak. But we, who go to church once a year, have nothing to say. What are we supposed to tell the world on this night? That we are against hunger, poverty and war? The pastor too had nothing to say. Thank God there were the prayers, that wonderful form of pausing through repetition that forces you to pay attention and yet allows you the feeling of freedom. I should write prayers, I thought, even if they would never meet the approval of my editor. A long prayer for the world. And then there were the songs, of course.

My neighbour on the pew was also my neighbour in the village, an apparently successful businessman who produced sheet metal as if the world could only be saved by sheet metal—that's what he said. His wife, with whom I occasionally discussed flowers, had died a short time previously. Cancer. The children were selling sheet metal and spending Christmas in California and Brazil, countries that were among his best customers. He was producing more than ever because the car industry in America had recovered. He had to build new factories and create lots of new jobs. He was worried about the strength of the euro. It's extraordinary that in a church, in sight of our Lord, someone should be whispering his concerns about the euro. We should watch out, was his motto, which naturally drew me into speculations about global financial markets. It was thanks to him that the statue of Christ in the church had been restored. He had donated a swimming pool and the sculpture for the village square and was well known for his generosity. He was visibly relieved when I accepted his offer to help consume the goose and made the strange remark that I did not have to say anything if I wasn't in the mood. As we said goodbye outside his house, he explained that, at too many official meals, he had sat next to people who had nothing to say and knew the embarrassment when one was forced to say something out of politeness. Since his wife had died, he had learnt to be silent.

His housekeeper, who had been with us in the church and walked home three steps behind us, roasted a wonderful goose, from Poland, and we drank the best red wine, that he produced himself, and talked about God and the world; and while we talked, the idea came to me that, if I were to write a new version of my novel, he would be the perfect patriarch, gathering his children around him in order to learn about the fate of his fortune and his firm. What kind of person would I be, I thought to myself while he described the power struggle with his brothers who wanted to drive him out of the company, were I to turn this man, who had so generously and so readily invited me to share his goose, into a fictional character just so that I could exploit him for my own benefit? On the other hand, he pretty much demanded that I do that very thing—whenever the talk turned to his brothers, he exclaimed that I should write his story down, he would leave it to me on his death, free of charge, because it was the history of the economic ascent of West Germany. I talk, you write, he cried, but you'll have to change the names or my brothers will take you to court, and you'll lose. sheet metal was the real motive force behind economic growth. Without sheet metal, there would be no successful health insurance, no social insurance, nothing. Not even synthetics had been able to push sheet metal aside. sheet metal is the winner of history. And if Africa—your Africa, he said, your Africa!—is ever to find peace, which would take decades, of course, then it would be sheet metal that did it. Africans are keen on sheet metal cars, he shouted to me across the long table, his cheeks full, and because Africans had oil and rare minerals they would be happy to exchange them for cars. When all Africans have cars, which, as I say, is only a question of a few decades, then my mission will be complete, was the conclusion of his long, beautiful speech, at the end of which he asked me to take care of peace in Africa. Who will do that, if not you? Instead of sitting in your garden listening to Mahler so loudly that the birds have to quit the village, you should go to Africa and fight for peace. You can be sure of my support.

As I had now definitively given up on any plan of writing my novel, I thanked my host for giving me an extra two years' lifespan. He was amazed at how long it took to write a book. Two years! he said with a look of concern. In two years, the world will have changed its face three times. While you sit there describing the face of the world, it will already have lost it, a terrible prospect! But as if to celebrate the, for him at least, incomprehensible extension of my lifespan, he invited me into his sauna. We sat for hours in his damp, warm vault and afterwards ate what was left of the goose, drank another bottle of his red wine and parted as friends. On his doorstep he told me that he had never met a writer in his life, only terrible salesman with quite obvious intentions, and the fact that he had helped the writer to no longer have to write filled him with pride and gratitude.

5

Dagmar arrived on 11 February. It had snowed the night before, so I could see her VW coming over the hill, like a red insect fighting its way through the drifts. In a thick fur coat of the kind shepherds wear in this area, a fur hat and fur boots, she looked as if she were heading off on an Antarctic expedition. But she looked anything but adventurous under all that clothing: she had lost weight and her face was pale and sunken. Her energetic walk had become a shuffle. I had always admired how she put her heel down first and then rolled her foot. Now it looked as if she was pushing her feet along in front of her. The moment she entered my little summerhouse, I had forgiven her. We were even. I would not write, she would give the purloined excerpts back and our life would continue on its easy way.

Now, I thought, as she switched the lights on, now she will discover the journal I had ostentatiously left open on the table, now she will sit down, red with shame, now she will put her head in her hands and begin to weep.

When she didn't reappear by afternoon and a light hadn't appeared in her window by twilight, I became uneasy. Everyone assumed that I was no good at comforting people because I didn't know how to look after myself. Nobody thought about comforting me. Dagmar forced me to go to her, when the right thing would have been for her to come to me. Perhaps they had different conventions in the North, where she came from.

I was angry with myself for thinking such a thing. She was obviously not well, so it was down to me to make the first approach. But what should I say? Nice to see you again? How are things at home? I couldn't start making accusations the second I had said hello! I couldn't tell her, as soon as I greeted her, that I felt that she had gone behind my back. Any moodiness on my part was probably inappropriate and so I determined to go and see her in silence, like an unbidden guest, to sit down and wait until she started to speak. But what if she remained stubbornly silent?

I knocked and went in without being asked. Dagmar lay in bed, her eyes open and her excerise book lying on her chest. To be exact, her eyes were wide open and tears flowed from them almost without interruption, running down past her ears and onto the pillow she had pulled out from underneath the bedclothes. Like a rare and beautiful stone with a spring within her that has been dried up for a long time. She lay there, motionless, her fur coat draped over her legs, the not-particularly-elegant Lapp-style boots still on her large feet and her fur hat on the table, where the book had been. Her beautiful hands, always rough, as if they had been scrubbed with hard soap, lay, like the hands of a military cadet, pressed neatly on her thighs.

She said nothing and I said nothing. What was I supposed to say? There was nothing to say. I had constructed an image of her that I needed to let go and now a person lay before me who was nothing like the Dagmar I had got to know. How was I to separate myself from the person before me and with what justification? I went to her, rolled her carefully to one side and lay down next to her. We lay there like an old married couple waiting for death and when the silent tears, that seemed like an emptying, finally stopped, she fell asleep.

In the night I left her and went back to my house. It was snowing again and the traces I'd left in the snow looked gigantic in the moonlight, as if a bear had walked through the garden deliberately leaving footprints behind.

The next morning, one of those indescribably beautiful mornings that are customary here, I saw through the window that she was packing her things into her car which, I now noticed, was already full to the brim with suitcases and bags, as if she had arrived intending to stay forever.

She drove away without a word.

When I later went into the summerhouse in order to think about her, I found a note on the table. It was torn out of a journal and was not a goodbye note. On it was written: I wanted to help you. I took the excerpts from your journals to show you that you were on the wrong track. But you can't be helped because you won't allow yourself to be helped. A writer's disease. Farewell and think of me occasionally. D.

When I rang my publisher later, completely distraught, and asked for Dagmar, he told me in a cheery voice that she had given in her notice with the intention of starting a new life in the south of Germany. I assumed, he laughed, that she was coming to you and I was concerned for you but obviously you've made another lucky escape.

I made a list of the things I wanted to do that day:

– ask the cleaning lady to tidy up the summer-house;

– inform the neighbours;

– phone the antiquarian in Stuttgart and tell him that he should come and get the books.

DINNER PARTY

Guests have been invited this evening for dinner;
there was no putting it off any longer. Over the
last few years, I had accepted four or five dinner
invitations (against both my will and better judgement), all of which ended up exactly as I had
imagined. There are people who can, with no
effort, sit at a stranger's table and entertain themselves and others brilliantly: I cannot. I once
caught sight of Schubert's wife in a mirror, making
faces at her businessman husband, that he should
rescue her from a bore like me. She was used to a
different calibre of guest, people who paid court
to her. I had nothing to say to her—I found her
almost repulsive in her beauty. Her husband, with
whom she changed places in order to escape my
company, was no better. He was a seriously rich
industrialist but couldn't tell me what drove him
to make his money. That is my job, he answered
curtly, to get rich and keep getting richer. He

bought his wife very expensive works of art for her birthday and was, even as he presented them to her, rubbing his hands with glee as he calculated the ten-fold return he would get when he sold them again in five years. And then? I asked. What do you mean—and then? He replied. Then if everything goes well, I'll have an extra five or six million in the bank. There were very beautiful pictures on the Schuberts' walls.

If everything goes well. What could possibly go well? The Schuberts came to dinner. And old Professor Mecken, whose wife had died that summer. That's the end of forty years of subjugation, he said to me, beaming with joy, as we drank a glass of wine in my garden after the funeral. He wanted to go travelling, see countries in which his wife would never have set foot and fall in love again. *Prof emer., young at heart, own house, financially independent, seeks female companion for travel to India. Preferably younger.* That was the ad he had placed in all the newspapers. He received almost two hundred replies, and, because he was a terrible pedant but also because he enjoyed the erotic frisson, he answered every one of them. One evening he came to me, clutching ten letters, completely exhausted with the effort of staving off the erotic flood that had broken over him and which, in truth, he had called down on himself; he laid the letters and accompanying photographs on the table and asked for my advice.

You can scarcely credit the arguments people can cook up for needing to go India: spiritual enlightenment, experience of unknown religions, finding themselves. None of them wrote that they wanted to get their hands on the old man's money; none of them asked how much he had in his bank account. I suggested that he invite all ten of the vultures at the same time and see which of them came out on top. But he was too cowardly for this, too much of an economic statistician and married for too long to allow that sort of farewell party. He invited them one at a time, put them through their paces one at a time, and one at a time rejected them all. And then he came moaning to me that he should have invited all two hundred in order to get a better overview. He cut a ridiculous figure.

Now, instead of going to India, he goes to Bad Gastein every year, to the spa, in order to rejuvenate himself. He writes articles for *festschrifts* in the hope that he will be able to hold onto his position in the academic world a little longer. In order to cheer him up a little, I had also invited Charlotte Beer, the widow of an art historian who would seek the meaning of life after three glasses, begin to cry after four and sing after five. She knows all the hits of the 1960s by heart, as if they were scratched onto a hard disk, and the fifth glass of wine is the switch that sets her off. Everyone looks askance when she pours herself a third glass, tries to console her after the fourth, when the sorrow of the world threatens to engulf her, and then turns away with an embarrassed look when she raises the fifth to her lips. A well-meaning woman, a bit too vulgar for the petty-bourgeois circles we move in but ideal for the professor, as she needs a strong shoulder when she is in a state of inebriation and he is only too happy to provide it. I have witnessed this peculiar couple more than once: an elderly woman drunk on the lap of an even more elderly economic statistician who is smiling inanely and seems to be looking for praise.

Finally, there are the Kleinschmidts, who always arrive with their daughter in tow, in the hope that they will find a good match for her at last. Herr Kleinschmidt belongs to that lucky few who, as members of the supervisory boards of companies, use their inside knowledge to make millions on the stock market. He was fired, of course, but was allowed to keep the money, which, in any case was already in his greedy wife's hands; who, in turn, had given it to Herr Schubert to look after and invest. Somehow, it was impossible to convert the daughter into cash. Nobody was willing to make an offer. No one wanted to take her on. She had been on the books for forty years, and cost them a tidy sum, as Herr Kleinschmidt called it, when, in her presence, he had quickly summarized what was owed to him: if you reckon two thousand euros a month, that makes twenty-four a year. On top of that you have travel, car, extras, so about fifty, and that times forty, then you'll have some idea what I'm talking about.

The daughter occupied herself looking after the animals she kept in the garden against her father's will. At night I could hear them howling. Once she asked me to help her bury one of them. I sat next to her in the passenger seat with the corpse, wrapped in an expensive scarf, on my knees. It was big as a calf, and, while she was busy looking for a particular path in the woods, I surreptitiously prodded the body to find out what it might have been. When, at long last, we came to the spot where the creature was supposed to find its resting place, I had the impression that something was moving under the cloth, as if the animal was sending some kind of signal from the other side. Don't let that disturb you, said Herr Kleinschmidt's daughter, that is its soul passing on a secret message to you that you should keep to yourself at all costs. When we had finally finished filling in the grave, covered in sweat, the Kleinschmidt daughter, whose first name I could never remember, gave a moving eulogy about the departed beast; while she spoke, I felt her hand creep into mine. A raw, cracked claw which must have experienced many such burials. We stood there hand in hand, sobbing, and any attempt I made to leave before the grieving came to an end made absolutely no impression.

For dinner it was roulades, though none of the guests seemed keen. I am happy to confess that I am not a particularly good cook and there was no need to tell me, as Frau Schubert did, that the sauce was an utter failure. The Kleinschmidts pushed the roulade to the side of their respective plates and Frau Kleinschmidt even tipped hers onto the tablecloth, making no particular effort to pick it up again. No one wanted to have anything to do with the roulade and it lay there, quite patiently, in its utter failure of a sauce.

The whole evening was taken up with talk of money: the money one had and the money that was still in the possession of others. At one point Schubert, in order to demonstrate something, reached over the table and grabbed his wife's string of pearls, which, as if it had just been waiting for this moment, fell apart immediately. A short time later, all of us, apart from the Kleinschmidt daughter, were on our hands and knees in the kitchen, trying to retrieve the pearls which had performed a rather successful vanishing act. We found all sorts of things that probably wouldn't have seen the light of day until after my death, were it not for this, but we didn't find the last two of the forty-two pearls belonging to the necklace. Frau Schubert accused Charlotte Beer of theft; Frau Beer, who had just lifted glass number five to her lips and was already belting out a German song at the top of her voice, was made to undress.

Professor Mecken, who seemed to know about her clothes, was asked to assist. Frau Beer then sat, more or less naked, at my kitchen table and had to be coaxed into finishing her song. Nobody mentioned the two missing pearls again but you could see Frau Schubert was still wracked with suspicion.

The evening dragged on like a never-ending torture; night came, dawn broke, and sent a doubtless short-lived light into my kitchen.

When all the guests had finally left, I took the almost untouched roulade and threw it over the fence into the Kleinschmidts' garden. The howling with which the creatures fell upon the meat will remain with me for the rest of my days.

IN THE MOUNTAINS

Once I followed the false ringing of the night bell—
now there's no way back.

Franz Kafka

I had gone out early to experience the sunrise, because, in my guesthouse down in the valley, I only ever became conscious of it after nine when, from my bed, the whole window suddenly seems to be ablaze and even the thick curtains cannot block out the light. The owner had made some sandwiches for me, so that, as she said, even if there were a blizzard I would be able to hold out for a week, although in this area and at this time of year, naturally, one would be lucky to escape alive. Just last week, she continued, taking obvious pleasure in regaling the world with such grim tit-bits, two English women had been caught out: stick-thin women who had been snapped like matchsticks in an avalanche. The landlady had been obliged to pack the English women's worldly goods—a collection of right tat!—and send them back to Britain without the slightest hope that she would be reimbursed for the postage. Whenever she said 'English women', she waved her arms around in the air as if she wanted to drive the spirits of those poor creatures out of her kitchen. The kitchen was full of spirits anyway, and always smelt of washing-up. I had to write my brother's telephone number down for her so that if things turned out badly—if you're torn apart by wolves—she would know who to contact. Who to contact? I hadn't seen my brother for decades; he'd emigrated to Australia, and I imagined his face—bloated with drink—on being told I had been torn apart by wolves. When our parents committed suicide, he lost all purpose in life; completely without direction, he was a spinning compass that could find no magnetic North. In Australia, the ethnologist was ostensibly studying the customs of the aborigines but found that he never got beyond their favourite pastime, namely, drinking. He wrote implacable, sorrowful letters to me from his village that sounded as though he had lost his skin and was vulnerable to everything around him—wind, weather, opinions and words. Everything he encountered found him defenceless and set about destroying his innermost being as if it had become the target of the termites that were gradually demolishing his hut.

In any case, he was no longer able, at least as far as I could judge from this distance, to board an aircraft. So I wrote down my brother's unfeasibly long telephone number on a serviette with a trembling hand as my broad-hipped landlady—who complained bitterly about wickedness in the world while seemingly content to appear as a personification of wickedness herself—watched over me. Then she, Frau Fuchs (widow Fuchs, to be precise, her husband had drunk himself to death) ripped it from me with her fat fingers and tucked into her overall which she wore every day as a form of personally tailored armour. I suddenly had the feeling that I had written down my own death sentence.

By eight I was halfway up the mountain. The paths had been cleared by the piste caterpillars which one could see at night moving across the slopes like humming fireflies. Suddenly, as if it had been tossed into the air by a boisterous god, the sun was standing high above the mountain opposite, opening up the view. My internal darkness of doubt and depression lifted too. Whereas just a moment before I had been nothing but a wheezing, sweating dot inching his way across this snow-covered stony desert, now I was a visible moving object, and immediately attracted the interest of the birds. Of course, it was the clever crows who announced my early intrusion into their territory to anyone who cared to know.

Crows will likely be the last living things on our planet. They teetered stiffly across the crust of snow with their tattered feathers, nodding to each other as if they were ticking off names on a list in their heads, and then hauled themselves upwards to follow the intruder from above. They sew a cloak for the landscape with black thread, and, when it is ready, let it drop suddenly and smother everything that is not able to get to safety. Everything, including me.

I am not a man of the mountains as such. I have resisted them for many years without really being able to justify my position. But now, accompanied by this overwhelming silence which even the crows could not disturb, the mountains were taking pains to drive the fear from my heart. During my working years, I had always gone to the coast for my holidays, at first to the Baltic and then, more and more frequently, to a Greek island. A school friend had left me a rundown fisherman's cottage next to the sea and the smell of it followed me all year. I only have to think of the house and I can smell the acrid stink of rotting fish in the heat, an aggressively pungent combination that, even in my memory, has a strangely calming effect on me. I can picture myself sitting on a wobbly wicker chair in front of the hut at the edge of the sea as it stretches glittering before me. I was always the only spectator of this natural spectacle in which nothing happened, apart from the shadow of the gods occasionally darkening the water and then lifting again, just as it should be when the gods are at play. As I sat there in front of my ocean, surrounded by this sacred stillness, a sense of bright joy often came over me and I felt as if I had been turned to stone, fixed to the spot, unable to move. This overwhelming feeling left me no choice: I had to submit to the sense of time dictated by its strange spell. It was only at sundown that I was able to free myself, when the contract I had made with the sea was fulfilled. The greatest gift I received, however, from simply sitting silently with the sea, was that after a few days there was a noticeable reduction in those needs, by which I, as someone who likes to think they can get by with the bare minimum, am nevertheless plagued. I needed almost nothing. I sat in silence, looking at the sea, and smoking. Even the most noble thought hesitated to disturb such a simple, such a pure, relationship. Sometimes I thought: now I can just dissolve and the next wave will carry me away.

Nothing will remain of those who live by the sea, not even a little pile of ash. This lesson I learnt soon after arriving at this magical place. It is not clear what secret switch was thrown to make human beings born in similar situations into such monsters of need, who feel that they have a right to everything; though any talk of the indeterminate nature of human character is not sufficient to describe the terrible consequences for our so-called civilization. But it was wise to avoid the tourists who had occupied the island's villages and beaches. In the evening, I would grill the fish Michalis had left on my doorstep that morning on an open fire, little red bodies dried out by the flames. Occasionally there would be an octopus that the fisherman would beat against the house walls as if its death was supposed to waken the dead. By the light of an unreliable lamp I read the great books, which, in the true sense of the word, became intelligible for me in that place. Or I listened to my friend Nicola, an Italian who had emigrated to America and had a house in the village that he occupied for the summer; he would come round in the evenings to recite the *Divine Comedy* from memory in a Florentine dialect, keeping rhythm, as it were, with the waves that got smaller and smaller as the night wore on, and which barely managed to drag themselves over the pebbles to the land and then disappeared again with a crunching sound.

I would never have left my place by the sea if on a memorably beautiful day the sea had not washed up a body at my feet: the corpse of an American woman who lived close to the village in a sheep stall and made her living by making and selling little chains and amulets stamped out of tin. In a world of haste, she was almost a monument to habit. There were no electrical machines allowed in her workshop, she had no car, not even a Vespa. She dressed conspicuously in layers of fluttering cloth, which, when the Estesian winds arrived on the island, blew out and billowed in all directions, so that as she came down the hill to visit me she looked like a brightly coloured bride of the wind. Then with a single movement she let all the fluttering veils fall away from her and strode, naked as a goddess, into the sea. Afterwards, she would drink a glass of wine with me. I soon tired of her esoteric talk, though. She had total command of the rhetoric of kitsch that was passed down from generation to generation of dropouts who spent a large part of the year living in the tumbledown sheep stalls on the island and which, as it was passed on, became thinner and more hollow until it finally consisted only of tasteless platitudes. But she was helpful and friendly and there was no reason to give her the cold shoulder as she passed through my land to the sea. I didn't even know her name.

But then the little waves nudged this woman's body towards my hut, a bloated Medusa whose veils danced on the water. I had to drag the slippery corpse onto land, run to the village and notify the police, get a doctor and hold back the growing numbers of onlookers, who, with arrogant nonchalance, trampled across the herb garden I had planted with such care, to reach my house, the house of a murderer, as I was soon called. Shortly after, the house was pulled down because there was rumoured to be a curse on it and nobody wanted to rent it. The American woman, the daughter of a well-to-do family—of course—was not, as we had all feared, taken back to America but buried in the cemetery with the whole village in attendance. Because her death and the circumstances that had led to it were the subject of interest in America too, people hoped—as I heard from my friend Michalis, the fishermen, who stayed true to me through the difficult months after—for well-heeled customers from the States, who, indeed, began to arrive shortly after.

Since then I have avoided the sea and taken every opportunity to travel into the mountains where, as God knows, other gods are in charge, even if their laws are no less hostile to humans. I became a mountain dweller.

*

After climbing another 20 metres up the slope, the official path came to an end. I stood, my heart beating, at a red-and-white-white barrier that blocked my way: danger of avalanches. But there was no way I could go back. It had taken everything out of me to climb this far, even if only to prove to myself that I was not past it. In any case, I had a goal. I wanted to find the houses and huts on the southern slopes of the mountain, only occupied in the summer months that I had visited some twenty years previously. Perhaps one places too much value on such memories which are generally of little substance: a view, a certain smell of summer that is brought about by the evening sun falling on wood and hay, an indefinable feeling of happiness that does not leave the body, even after decades have passed. I could name ten such places connected to the most peaceful and richest of memories. In truth, I am made of these memories; the rest is just the junk that everyone carries around with them.

Back then, for sure, it had been summer: one of those indescribable summers in the mountains with an impossibly blue sky and blossoming meadows and a quality of air that makes one think life goes on for ever. I visited a mill in the valley that produced fabric on ancient looms and was listed in our catalogue under 'Excursions'. I was meant to write a blurb. Because the visit to the monosyllabic weavers was shorter than expected—they sat at their looms, their teeth clenched, and said nothing—I stayed for a long weekend in the only guesthouse in the lonely little village. And, as soon as I had written my report about the silent men and their extraordinary fabrics, I set off on a programme of walks. It was on one of these that I saw in the distance, yet still within reach, or so it seemed, a group of houses that appeared to have been thrown beyond the treeline, up where the mountain started, as if by God's hand, and I decided at once that I would make these houses my journey's goal. My Jerusalem, I said to myself, and was quite sure that something significant would happen to me.

What at first looked like an hour's walk soon turned out to be much longer on account of the frequent zigzagging of the path which seemed to go on for ever, even though the houses appeared to be just around every corner. Although the landlady of the guesthouse had assured me that I would be the only walker and therefore have to take extra care not to fall, because the mountain rescue would have difficulty reaching me, I glimpsed a woman ahead of me on a straight section, who— I could tell because the distance between us was growing with every step—was walking at a much faster pace. Probably a dairy maid, I thought, visiting her husband in the summer meadow. Before the final curve, when I was at last sure that I had got past the deceptive vistas, I saw her sitting in front of one of the huts. She waved at me. And because her gesture can have been intended for no one but me in this sublimely lonely place, I waved back, at first hesitantly and somehow clumsily but then with more confidence, like someone who had never waved before and was only now discovering endless pleasure in it. I repeated this gesture several times as if to reassure myself that the stranger would not suddenly get up and carry on, leaving behind only the memory of a single greeting. But she had no intention of disappearing. As I got closer, I saw that she was wearing leather knee-breeches and bulky mountain boots, and that a tightly packed rucksack was leaning against the wall next to her. Around her throat was a red cloth that was so thin that from a distance it looked like a collar separating her head from her body. She had tried to contain her sweeping mane of dark brown hair with a clasp at the back of her head but my first impression, of meeting a Medusa, would not go away, even when I was standing in front of her and attempting to introduce myself. This impression was enhanced when she lifted her head and pressed it against the wooden wall of the hut. Whether it was because I was out of breath after the climb or the presence of the woman had disturbed me, I mumbled my name as if I wasn't quite sure whether it was mine or not, which made the woman ask me to spell it. No sooner than I had done so, for good or ill and with much stuttering, she said, 'Sit down. Life is too short to spend it standing up,' which, when the rucksack had been moved from the narrow bench, I did.

The third sentence this unusual woman spoke to me was no less strange than the second, which I mulled over for some time because I couldn't decide whether it was correct: that the short span of life is better spent sitting than standing, or even walking. Sometimes I conclude that I have walked far too much and not sat down enough and then, sometimes the opposite: it is clear that there is no ideal balance between the two. The third sentence, spoken after a long pause, was a question: 'Did you bump into my husband?' I was far too shocked too tell the truth and mumbled something along the lines of 'I don't think so,' in order to leave myself some room for manoeuvre, because in fact I had immediately thought of answering 'Yes' in order to test the veracity of the question. Did she have a husband at all, or was the question meant as a warning, in the sense that if I were to touch her, he might jump out from behind a rock? Of course I could have just retorted: yes, he is standing in front of you! But I had never managed this level of brazenness in my life.

Before anything else was said, the beautiful woman took off her blouse, the heavy shoes and then the leather breeches, and took out the most delicious food from her rucksack—hard-boiled eggs, sausage, tomatoes and cucumber. Lightly dressed as she was, she collected fresh spring water in her canteen and invited me to join her for a snack. She used a dialect word that I don't think had ever crossed my lips until that moment. With a hunger that surprised me, I fell upon the food now laid out on her red neck-cloth, and, after a few minutes, was clearing up the last crumbs of bread with my middle finger, finishing off every-thing she had offered. By way of concluding this extraordinary feast, she produced a hip flask of fruit schnapps. Because the husband had not turned up, either in real life or in her conversation, I agreed with her suggestion that we take a little nap in the shade of the hut. Before too long I fell deeply asleep and experienced a sense of well-being greater than I had ever felt in my life. When I awoke, the sun had gone down and the woman had disappeared. I tried to recall every word she had said to me so as to glean some sense of her life; but aside from the fact that she was a politically engaged social worker from Geneva, I could remember nothing. She slipped into my life like a shadow, but one that left a deep impression; one that would never leave me in all the following years.

*

And now I was back on my way to this place, even if the conditions en route were completely different. But something drove me to fight through the snow, whatever the cost.

'If you make it,' a solemn inner voice had said to me a few days previously, 'you will be safe for now.' I was particularly susceptible to such messages at that moment because the firm for which I had worked as a subcontractor, writing its catalogues for the last twenty years, had decided to find a replacement for me without giving me any notice. How and where had they found him? And why were they looking for a replacement anyway? We, or rather, the firm, was the leading fabric merchant in Europe, and twice a year I would write texts for its compendious catalogues, including short entries on Indian weaving culture and brilliant essays on English wools, dotted with literary quotations. Forty catalogues, six thousand pages. That was my life's work, and it had been brought to an abrupt end. I had never thought about looking for other commissions. It gave me such pleasure to provide cashmere with new nuances or to praise the qualities of rare linens that when I was fired I felt life had let me down at a decisive moment. At the same time, I have to admit that I never expected anything else. The new boss, a smart young man, did not even have the decency to let me know about my dismissal in person, but left it to Human Resources to tell me that they had decided to take on a more 'modern' copywriter in order to 'stabilize' the future of the business. It brought little comfort to hear from all my former customers that they missed my 'educated' essays; nor did I take any secret pleasure in the rumours, that soon became certainty, that the business was haemorrhaging money because people were buying fabric directly over the Internet and not from wholesalers.

In any case I now had more time to head off on my travels.

With great effort I climbed over the red-and-white barrier and trudged through the deep, glistening snow towards the woods. The path became visible again as soon as I reached the first bare larches. I stood for a long time looking at the larch needles that shone red in the early light and made strange patterns on the snow, as if someone had set them out especially for me. As I was standing there, half in the warming sun, half in the icy shadow of the trees, I suddenly saw two deer heads gaping at me from a pile of snow. I pushed the snow aside with my foot and saw the skeletons and, further up the hill, the bloody innards, frozen solid. I covered the dead animals' eyes with snow, bending as I did so because I thought it indelicate to drop it from above. What I had seen was hardly good preparation for climbing the Maiensäss mountain pasture. A short while ago, the exertions of the climb had been very tempting, like some kind of purification, but now the dead eyes followed my every step. Should I turn around and inform the police?

I quickly went on my way, albeit now no longer easy of mind. In the forest, which now seemed like a mortuary chapel after the sight of the dead eyes of the deer, I could hear my heart beating in the silence. I could see the path, but every few metres I had to climb over encrusted snowdrifts or frozen streams and I was constantly afraid of falling into a bottomless abyss. Grey icicles hung from the rock wall to my right and I held onto them, trembling, until they broke.

I did lose my balance once. A huge waterfall behind a wall of ice tumbled down into a temporary pool, from which the water crashed down over the path and on down the mountain. Around the pool and the narrow bridge made of only three planks, everything was iced over, and, already with my first step, I began to slip and slide towards a gap that now, in winter, in the absence of the protective clothing of luxuriant vegetation, showed quite clearly what was awaiting me: a fall of hundreds of feet down the mountainside, over rocks and logs. Suddenly I was sitting above the foaming waters, whose unknown source was somewhere above me and whose power was attempting to rob me of my senses, with the single perpendicular bridge support between my legs. Despite the wetness and the fear that had shot through my body when I had fallen and despite the pain I could feel in my back—made worse by the cold—I observed with absolute calm how the great glazed boulders made the churning water pause for a moment before falling inevitably into the abyss. All the thoughts that followed were prefixed by: if I survive this . . . , thus proving that I wanted to survive, even if, during those eternal minutes in the ice, I had been able to picture myself falling with the water. I had lived my life and there was no reason, at my age, to hope for a few 'golden years' at the end. The euphemistic way that age tends to be described, as bringing in the harvest, is pitiful; the terrors of death need no metaphorical watering down. One simply disappeared. And if that bridge support had not been there between my legs when I came to grief on the wafer-thin layer of ice that covered the rocks, no one would have heard my last calls.

But I would not have been able to write this report if I had not been able to scramble to my feet. Nevertheless, the world, the colours of the world, had changed for good. The things that become visible in the snow often have a deep significance. Now they had lost some of their brilliance.

I had been walking for some four hours on this complicated and arduous—in all senses of the word—journey when, finally, midday being long past, I saw in the distance the empty wooden houses of my Jerusalem. In a further two hours I managed to reach them, soaked through and joints aching. There were eight houses spread out along the slope. I recognized 'my' house straightaway, alongside two large barns that functioned as shelters for sheep in the summer storms and a chapel that was so small that only one penitent at a time could enter.

I was overcome by a heavenly calm. I had made it.

As I approached, I saw a man, crouching, wrapped up in thick layers of garments. He looked like a tent. He'd obviously been watching me for some time, otherwise he would have given some sort of sign of being surprised by such an unexpected guest. But he seemed so sure of himself that he didn't even look up. Wolves probably, he muttered, as I stood beside him. He was using a blue plastic comb, like the ones given as a consolation prize at a fairground, to measure the size of the clearly visible tracks and then photographing them. They couldn't be badger, nor wild boar and there are no dogs here, so they'll probably be wolves. Are you a hunter too? Got a rifle with you, he asked still crouching and without wasting so much as a glance on me.

I tried to get past him but it was impossible, as much on account of the towering snowdrifts as the man's barked comments. Each word was like a brick in a solid wall that one could only have got over with a giant leap. But who can take a giant leap in the snow?

I remained silent. I always remained silent when there was nothing to say, rather than try to talk my way out, as one learnt at school and in later life, so that most people tried to do it all the time. This unbearable tendency to try and talk one's way out of things had become the basis of what we call conversation. Its emaciated form can be found in the discussions on television, which are a constant talking one's way out of things in order to fill time, because at some point a law was passed that made talking compulsory. The legislator was society as a whole. Sometimes I imagined a silent society, a community living in monastic silence and communicating only with signs. Talking would be permitted for three weeks a year, in the holidays, and then we would realize how we all squeeze ourselves dry to the point of exhaustion. Day and night we talk, we argue, we shout and then there is silence.

And so I kept quiet, which probably didn't improve my situation. Because I wasn't able to fix my gaze on the tracks that had allegedly been made by a wolf, I looked around at the sublime landscape: clouds had now come up from the south and the sun had all but disappeared, shining only on a few mountaintops in the west, as if trying to find its orientation. It would soon get very dark and it was terribly cold.

No smoke came from any of the houses so I had no idea in which of these constructions, distorted by the wind, the mysterious man at my feet lived, or whether he lived in this godforsaken place—which was of course anything but forsaken by God—at all.

It has to be a wolf. Nothing else makes any sense, the man growled, still crouching. He put the blue children's comb and the tiny camera into one of the many pockets in his anorak and made to get up. He had been crouching for so long that his legs did not seem to work and he stretched his hand out to me, which, after some hesitation, I took. Naturally I wasn't obliged to take his hand; I might have kicked him without warning, kicked him all the way down the slope and watched him roll down so that nothing was left of him but scraps for the foxes. But I grabbed his hands and pulled so that he grew in stature and height, looming ever larger, and, when I pulled him back up into life with one final tug, he blundered clumsily towards me and fell into my arms and we found ourselves once again in the snow. There was no word of apology. No embarrassing mumbling. He lay on me with the full weight of his life, his breath heavy and warm in my face. His eyes were so close to mine I thought I could see myself reflected in them. I saw the deep, dark furrows around them that reminded me of my grandfather on my father's side, who drank himself to death in sorrow. How, when and why such sorrow had found its way into him, he would never reveal, he said, because he didn't want to burden us. But one could see from the black lines etched around his eyes that seemed to grow ever darker, how great the sorrow was that drove him and how it sucked him dry until he was quite empty. In the end it only took one schnapps for him to be tipsy, a second and he was drunk, a third and he was dead.

Do you have a rifle with you? The hunter asked me once again. Without a rifle you'll not get off the mountain alive.

*

He had three rifles that he kept in his hut, the smallest hanging on the wall next to the stove. Just take one of them, he said, they're all loaded. Without us having introduced ourselves, he had asked me to follow him into his hut (the smallest of the group before us) because he was of the view that I would freeze to death outside. It would have been impossible to contradict him. The wolves are just waiting for someone like you! An ice-cold wind had come up, bringing with it more dark clouds so that the whole sublime panorama had disappeared as if by magic. Nevertheless, I toyed with the idea of heading back straight away because the thought of spending a whole afternoon and a night with this strange man in his hut, supposedly surrounded by wolves, scared me. But when I turned away from him to bid farewell, he jumped in front of me and pointed with some force in the direction of his hut. Then he grabbed hold of me from behind and pushed me towards his door. You're staying put, he whispered into my ear, we don't want to die. As if my life was anything to do with him!

We drank a schnapps and then laid a fire; as the room began to warm up and our breath no longer hung white in the air, he locked all the windows and both doors and began to prepare an evening meal. A hearty meal! he exclaimed. He told me to take off my wet clothes and put on some of his old trousers and a shirt I would find in the chest. As I stood in the corner of the kitchen, trembling with shame as I changed my clothes, standing on one leg and struggling with the over-long trousers of my host, I saw a one-eyed cat come into the warmth through its own little entrance and look me over with such curiosity that I completely lost my balance.

I had the feeling that he didn't know what to do with me. I'm not an adventurer who likes to boast with heroic tales, just as it is not my way to talk about women in crude terms, as was the case in his circles, and my interest in dead animals or the ways in which one can shoot them dead is limited. Nevertheless, now that it was clear I was not going to run away, we had to come to some sort of arrangement about how we would spend the night. When he heard what I had done with my life so far, and hoped to continue doing with a new employer if possible, he broke into ugly laughter that turned into a long cough and thence into a lump of phlegm that he spat into the stove without batting an eyelid. That can't be true. A whole life describing fabric? What a miserable life!

Was it? Maybe he only wanted to undermine me, make me look ridiculous, so that he could continue to demoralize me? My perhaps not-especially-common but in no way ridiculous style of describing certain things had sometimes mystified people but never prompted such scorn. Today—I said while he continued coughing—one simply takes these descriptions from the Internet, plays around with them a little and then publishes them without citing any sources, so that I often come across my words in descriptions of cashmere, even in translations. You could say that I have given cashmere its language.

You poor bugger, said my host. I promise you that from now on cashmere will never cross my threshold. As he said these words, he scrunched his dark eyes shut and began to laugh uproariously, as if he had told a great joke. You can rely on me, he screamed, as if he had lost his mind, cashmere is quite out of the question!

The room was dominated, or perhaps filled, with a dull, pungent smell that soaked into every object. If one pressed a glass to one's lips, or even a fork, the concentrate of smoke, sweat and blood assailed one's nostrils and one lost the will to move. I sat almost motionless and silent.

Was I afraid I might die?

We ate buckwheat spaghetti and drank a bottle of Bernese wine and the man, whose name was

Thomas, but who wanted to be called Tom, told me his life story, but in such a rambling way that, by the end of his miserable family saga, I had no clue who had died young, nor when, nor why. In all it was a story full of death. He had been one of eleven children, all of whom were now dead apart from him and one sister whom he wished dead anyway because she—the owner of a guesthouse—was rolling in money and had no children and could have given all her money to the nephews and nieces—those that were still alive at least—rather than the church. It cost such an effort to follow that it sent my entire being into spasms.

While Tom thrashed about in his death fantasies in a windowless room, whose walls were made of hatred, cynicism, despair and pomposity—rough, unplastered walls that one was well advised to avoid—I reflected on how it is possible to lose sight of light, lose sight of the light of happiness, of grace, of self-denial; the light of modesty, obedience and integrity. Everybody—regardless of intelligence or background or upbringing—dreams about one day receiving this light, feeling it on their skin or soul. In the first case, it enters from outside; in the second, it emerges from inside. In my case, I have always felt it first outside, on my skin, and then it finds its way inwards at various speeds until it reaches my soul. How often has that happened to me? Ten times, at the most.

Tom would entertain no such thoughts. He had no interest—and he said this several times—in dissipating the darkness inside him. He loved the secret, the brutal and the repulsive, and found little else worthwhile. He made no attempt to present himself as special in any way, not even as a particularly dissolute outsider seeking retribution for everything that had gone wrong in his life. He was quite content to present the less interesting picture of an average brute—part of the reason being that he had no wish to take any notice of me or understand me. He spoke, he commanded, he gave instructions, and I listened, silent and forlorn.

The two deer, back at the turning . . . , I ventured, intruding into his labyrinthine thoughts, as he was bent over adding wood to the fire and wasn't able to speak: yes, the deer, he answered, a hunter leaves the skeleton and the head for the foxes. To come back the subject of his sister, he added with a bleak laugh, he'd have nothing against her getting run over by a car.

He sat cheek by jowl with me on the bench, and, because I was right at one end, I couldn't move away from him and his curses. So I stood up, went around the table and sat down on the other side, although here I was in danger of being burnt by the hot stove. I should have laid down on the bench, then Tom would have been forced to draw the only chair up to the table. He had lit a stinking stub of a cigar and was occasionally blowing smoke into the cat's ears. The cat, lying on the table in front of him with its eyes closed, responded with a violent shake of its head but made no effort to get up.

After the meal, Tom fetched a box with a photo album containing photos of him with some of his trophies: in Canada, he had shot two bears and an elk. There were several photos of each of the three animals, all of which showed Tom, hands on hips, rifle slung over his shoulder, and his left foot on the dead bodies. The bear was this close to me, he shouted, red in the face from one too many schnapps, I only had to pull the trigger. As he said this, he dug his fingers in my ribs and said *peow peow* as if imitating the action of his repeater rifle. Poor old Mr Bruin got a bit of a shock, and so did his friend Pete who was accidentally shot by Canadian hunter a short time later and shut his eyes for good.

At a certain point, I couldn't bear listening to any more of the horror stories he had 'documented' in his album and which he was obviously intent on telling, so I asked if I might get some shut-eye until first light. You can't leave at dawn under any circumstances, he said coolly, you'll never get over the iced-up snow slopes or you'll slip and land in the valley by Thusis. There's a nice cemetery there with a few of us in it. He couldn't miss any opportunity, even something as innocuous as this, to add one of his malicious comments.

He wouldn't let me stretch out on the bench with my rucksack as a pillow. Instead, he pulled me up roughly and pushed me into a side room with two wooden bunk beds. You're on the bottom, he said, in my wife's bed. More than six years ago she . . . , but I interrupted him with such a loud voice that he actually stopped talking for a moment. He fetched a couple of furs from the corner—I shot them myself!—and threw them at me before going back into the kitchen where I saw him finish the last of the schnapps.

I found myself thinking of a note in Kafka's fragments that I have looked up in the meantime:

> The Czar's courier spent the night in a small steppe village and was already in bed, in the only room in the hut, with the peasant's family sleeping round him, a few goats huddled together in the corner, more restless than the people . . . The courier hardly slept. When on his travels he generally did not sleep at all, only when the situation seemed entirely safe did he close his eyes and go straight to sleep, but even then kept control of himself, so that noises did not wake him, but rather he listened out for them in his sleep, and anyway he

could not tolerate any sleep that lasted longer than quarter of an hour, but would wake himself up.

I didn't sleep for a second. I listened to the mice, who were obviously happy to have this unexpected visitor and were not afraid of the one-eyed cat. I heard every gust of wind and every creak; but above all I was glad when my host quickly fell into a noisy sleep. He claimed he had a job in the IT department in one of the towns in the valley but had been made redundant because IT was developing far too quickly, and, when he was asked what he thought should be done to catch up with it, he had replied that above all he would like to shoot the town council. He was immediately relieved of all his duties and was now living, for as long as possible, in his mountain hut, because his flat in town was occupied by his unemployed son with whom, as he put it, he did not see eye to eye. My son, he shouted, has a tendency to violent episodes.

And what about the wolves? Were they really wolf tracks?

I must have fallen asleep out of sheer exhaustion. When I opened my eyes the next morning, I found myself looking into the eyes of my host who was sitting on the edge of my bed and bending over me. His staring must have woken me. He was the first to look away. We ate the rest of the warmed-up spaghetti in silence, and then, while he went to see if there were any fresh tracks outside, I pulled on my dry clothes and got ready to leave. It was already gone ten o'clock. I was greeted outside the hut by bright sunshine. The whole valley was lit up and one could see right down to the motorway. Every so often an unnaturally large snowflake fell from the sky and its lustrous glitter only emphasized the sense of dazzling radiance.

But nothing was to be seen of Tom.

In panicked haste I set off for the path and made up my mind to send him a letter. The post would surely reach him even up here and perhaps I would include a little money as thanks for the awkward hospitality. I believe I have rarely felt as relieved as I did in that moment of my departure; for I was sure I would never have to see him again in my life.

An eternal flame burned in the little chapel. I looked in quickly in order to give thanks for my life. On a whitewashed ledge, next to a wooden crucifix, stood the photograph of a woman in a broken frame, who had lost her life on the mountain. I was certain that I recognized her.

The sun had already started to thaw the snow crust so I was able to make good progress. Just before the turning behind which the deer heads were waiting for me I paused for a moment and looked back like someone who has escaped one more time, even though I wondered what I was going to do with my life. I felt empty, lifeless. I closed my eyes so I would feel the sunlight on my eyelids and, sure enough, I felt them warming up.

I knew you'd find it difficult to tear yourself away, said Tom suddenly, so close behind me that I didn't even need to turn around. You can help me scatter the ashes.

He was carrying two buckets of ash to a wooden shed that stood, half-hidden by trees, further up the slope. We had to walk about a hundred metres uphill in the deep snow. In the shed were eight colonies of bees that he looked after. When the sun fell on the white of the open slope, he explained, the bees woke early from their hibernation and flew out into the whiteness. And were blinded. Blind bees give less honey, he said, and anyway it's animal cruelty. We began to scatter handfuls of ash on the ground around the shed. Because of the deep snow, it was hard work and we carried it out silently and doggedly. Once, when I looked into the window of the warped hut below, I saw, which no longer surprised me, someone else looking back.

I had, whatever might happen next, lost my life.

THE FUTURE

She left and was never seen again.

One could limit the account of a story to this—it is true enough.

We sat at the table eating dinner, drinking wine and telling stories about the old days, and now and again one of the young women would try to imagine a future, as if it were a straightforward business. There were five of us. Since there was a sixth chair at the table, the landlord, who had plenty of experience but kept himself to himself, occasionally joined us. He had a friendly face, or maybe he put on a friendly face, because sometimes I saw the way his mouth and eyes twitched when something went against the grain. I did not take a particularly lively part in the conversation, which took place for the most part between the other four who were all trying hard to find what they had experienced in the past interesting as well as mustering some semblance of interest in what was happening in the present but that was over as soon as it happened. Only the young woman who left and was never seen again insisted that she wanted to speak about the future because it seemed senseless to think of a past without a future. She had an oval face and expressive hands with which she gave a bodily form to all her ideas about the future. What do you mean? she asked me. I had the dubious reputation within this group of friends of being unapproachable, even though I sometimes forced myself to play the the life and soul of the party, the clown. But on this occasion I felt myself called upon to find the right words. I can well imagine having a future with you, I said, but, because I was the oldest in this group, I added: but I cannot see our future having much of a past.

I had spoken with such earnestness that the inappropriate laughter of the other three came only with a certain delay, lasted too long and then stopped suddenly. A silence fell upon us so huge and draining that it could no longer brook a friendship with those who had so brazenly laughed.

In the midst of this silence the young woman with the oval face stood up, and, without another word, left the restaurant.

Incomprehensibly, I stayed sitting in the present; with the others, but separated from them for ever, I lay my head in my hands and wanted to remain in this undiluted misery until the woman returned. But she was never seen again.

We turned the house upside down—it was the last thing we did together—searched the cellar, the attics, garages and business premises, and then decided to head off in the four directions of the compass to look for her. The two men headed off towards South and West; the woman was to explore North; and East fell to me. I kept firmly on track.

When at the close of my life I returned to the restaurant—the owners had renovated and installed a bowling alley and a swimming pool—with only a little future left before me, I looked up at the middle top window of the freshly rendered building and saw the young woman. She waved as if she had been waiting for me. With my last ounce of strength, I raised my hand and waved back.

RETURN FROM LEIDEN

I returned from Leiden, from my friend's funeral, and stood helplessly in room that was both my study and my bedroom; but I could think neither of work nor sleep. I was so beside myself that I couldn't even sit down, and the book I picked up at random—on the concept of the 'picaro'—did nothing to help me get over my anxiety. Up until I departed—fled the scene—I had felt I was witnessing my own funeral. I had been in the process of burying myself: my 'conscious-intentional-decision-making-self' seemed to be disintegrating before my very eyes, falling to pieces, turning to ash. And so, in full view of the bewildered mourners, I had rushed out with a loud scream and been taken directly to the airport.

I went to the window and clutched at the cold latch, my forehead pressed against the glass. Slowly, I was able to breathe properly again.

In my mind, I could see the house in which my friend had lived for more than thirty years: the kitchen, crammed with people dressed in black, chatting while they drank coffee and ate biscuits. I saw the old enamel sink with its large broken patch; I saw the crooked kitchen cupboard with its chaos of cutlery, a row of champagne bottles and piles of tatty books distorted with damp; 'Marcus Aurelius' and the *Divine Comedy* could be made out on the spines but there were also translations of my friend's own books. He had been particularly pleased with the Chinese versions of his most important works because, he erroneously believed, there was still a chance to 'get things moving' in China. Later he was deeply disappointed when it turned out that, aside from his name on the cover, there was very little of him to be found in the translations. From that moment on, China was 'dead' for him.

A beautiful, spacious kitchen, spoilt only by the crowds of funeral guests. They sat around the kitchen table like ravens, furtively watching one another. Who will be next? I had met an old kappelmeister, with a heart condition, whose breath whistled as he wheezed up the stairs; I dragged him up to the first floor where he lowered himself, creaking, onto an old trunk. He had somehow managed to get up to the second floor and was now sitting with bulging red eyes, nibbling biscuits at the kitchen table, a tumbler of champagne in his shaking hands. He was to give the official eulogy at the town hall later and asked me who he should mention.

The four wives were there, their children and their children's children and their new husbands; fellow writers, who secretly—you could see it on their faces—were thinking that they now had one fewer competitor when it came to the State Prize for Lifetime Achievement. There were museum people, politicians and several friends, a number of whom, in spite of the unfamiliar surroundings, I recalled having met before; a banker, for example, in whose car we had once driven to Antwerp, an unforgettable journey because this cheerful-looking man had to stop every five minutes to relieve a painful bladder. We arrived in Antwerp so late that night that we had to turn and drive straight back again—the gallery holding the exhibition opening we wanted to visit was already closed.

Two of the grandchildren had taken off their shirts and were showing each other their new tattoos, mythical symbols in a variety of colours scratched into their pale backs, and a politician's wife, whose head, heavy with age, was weighed down onto her chest by a massive gold necklace, traced the runes with an unbelieving finger, as if they were holy images.

I had first met my friend an age ago in Venice, in a tiny hotel behind La Fenice in which we had each rented a room on the third and top floor. He was staying in Room 302, I in 303 and in 301 a fat Cypriot art historian who had noticed that there was something wrong with the angels in Tiepolo's painting in San Rocco. This puffy sausage of a man would not tell us what because, as he said (word for word): 'My only sin is mistrust.' One evening, this emblem of mistrust got himself stuck in the lift door and was calling in such panic for help that we—I and the man who would later become my friend—shot out of our rooms to free the copiously sweating man and his full shopping bags from his cage. Breathing heavily, the three of us found ourselves cheek by jowl in the narrow hall, and, in the confusion caused by our untoward proximity, I went into 302, the Cypriot went into my room and my friend-to-be into the Cypriot's. Like a Venetian comedy, the Dutch man and I stood facing each other again in the hallway within seconds while the sweating art historian recovered from his horrors in my room. Nothing more was heard from him apart from the occasional sigh.

Having introduced ourselves, the Dutchman and I barged into the Cypriot's room so as to get a better impression of his work. The walls were covered with images of angels; in the middle hung a poster of 'Abraham Receiving the Three Angels' and, on the back of the door, angels coming to Hagar and Ishmael's rescue. Obviously he was occupied with researching the structure and form of angels' wings, or at least there were lots of calculations to that effect, and, if appearances did not deceive, was also an expert in esoteric knowledge. While I was inclined to treat the strange series of numbers and drawings in which the movement of angels and their rates of acceleration were calculated as complete balderdash, the Dutchman found some comfort in this numerology. He took out his little book and made notes in a tiny script, and later photographed the series of numbers: in order, he said, to compare them with his own.

When I left the kitchen and crept into my deceased friend's study, I saw enlarged photographs of the numbers hanging above his desk, covered with notes. I was about to study them more closely when suddenly the door to this silent room opened and four pall-bearers in frock coats and top hats entered, carrying their plain wooden box, and, without acknowledging me, headed towards the small room behind the monumental desk. I knew from earlier visits that my friend kept his favourite books in that room and read them there, and only there, lying on a couch. It was unimaginable that the four pall-bearers would be able to fit inside. I didn't have long to think about it because, seconds later, they burst out again, the wooden box tilted

at a perilous angle so that it could turn the corner
without hitting anything. My friend lay in that
casket. They laid him directly at my feet and leant
the lid against the desk. One of the pall-bearers,
now carrying his top hat in his hand, said, in
English, that I should say my goodbyes quickly so
that we could get to the service at the town hall
on time. He didn't want to be responsible for any
lateness. I was the only one in the room. The others were still sitting upstairs in the kitchen, and,
as an outsider, I didn't want to be the one to go
and chivvy them.

One of the pall-bearers sat in my friend's chair
and absentmindedly fiddled with the holy objects
on his desk. I almost stopped breathing when I
saw how blithely he played with the tiny shrunken
heads, those crumpled bags of skin which my
friend had assembled into quite a community over
the years, people about as big as a hand, with oval
eye sockets and a penis the size of a match, the
hair still firmly on their heads and unusually long,
torn fingernails. My dead friend had collected
this army of souls—at first guess, around thirty
gnomes, standing on thin metal discs along the
length of his desk—during his perilous journeys
through Africa and South America. Now they
watched over him, a fact which often led to him
say to say quite casually: if my demons will allow
it, or, I wonder what the gods of the writing desk
will have to say about that. The gods of the writing

desk, exclusively male as far as I remember, often did have different views about the quality of my friend's work which, as he explained to me, led to long and uncomfortable séances that did not always go in his favour. I was unable to find out anything more specific.

There was, however, one supreme law in this study, a condition that had to be met before one was permitted entry: one was not allowed to touch the demons, not even their flat bases, and certainly not the defenceless little bodies themselves, though one was certainly tempted to feel their crumpled skin. Another friend of mine, a historian from Leiden and world-renowned expert on heretic sects of the Spanish Middle Ages, who was always scathingly ironic when talk turned to my friend's demons, told me that our friend's dog, a huge royal poodle, once licked the skin of one of the little men and died a few days later of some kidney complaint.

Now one of the pall-bearers was slouching in my dead friend's chair and had one of the demons in his left hand. With the forefinger of his other, its nails nicotine yellow and bitten down almost to the quick, he dabbed shamelessly at the delicate little head as if testing how solid it was. I could see quite clearly what fate would befall him in the coming days. Until this moment he had been fit as a fiddle, had just smoked his last cigarette and started to exercise—and wasn't working in the fresh air a sign that he would live a long life? He will die, I told myself, but I could not bring myself to say a word, even to spare the man from the terrible torture I knew awaited him. The other pall-bearers sat on the sofa, their top hats on their knees, like a picture from the golden age of Dutch portraiture: 'The Guild of Funeral Directors'. And I stood looking down at my friend, dressed in his best suit.

In Venice, a few days after we had got to know each other, he admitted that he only came to the city on account of the tailors; and that all his suits and shirts, but also the light coats he wore, had been made in Venice; and because, in the course of the years, I got to see the great majority of these suits, shirts and light overcoats, I was in a better position to judge why this man had to go to Venice so often. I myself have never cultivated a taste for gentleman's couture. When I look at the photos from the last twenty years or so, taken at family funerals, I always see myself standing at a colourful graveside dressed in the same suit, a dark speck in an ocean of flowers. At a rough calculation I'd say that I have only worn my suit, which I still possess today, around forty times: to thirty funerals and about ten other events I am reluctant to think about. Obviously, my shape has not changed significantly while my friend, as I could see in his study in Leiden, only appeared to be about half his original bodyweight. Like a miniature copy of the original writer, he looked out from one of his more than forty Venetian suits as I stood over him in my only suit and stared down at him. His hands, flecked with liver spots, had been folded across his body, a position he would never have adopted during his lifetime, at least I can't imagine that he would have gone so peacefully to his grave.

Steps could be heard outside and soon the other funeral guests, some of them with bright red faces, entered the study. They had survived the descent down the dangerously narrow staircase despite the copious amounts of alcohol consumed. They paused for breath so as to prepare themselves for the last steps down to the exit. When they caught sight of their friend lying peacefully in his casket, they looked around as if they had been caught out, then sighed and went on their way. The four pall-bearers fixed the lid with a sort of clamp, heaved the casket onto their shoulders and, grunting and groaning, followed the guests. The coffin kept knocking against the bannisters or scraping against the ceiling and several times lurched so violently that I had to reach above their heads and grab hold of it to prevent a catastrophe. The thought that my friend would exit his last abode—albeit involuntarily—by tumbling down his confounded stairs one last time was comical and terrible at the same time. Comical because my friend, while he was alive, had the strangest views about death. Let's just say that for him burial was not the end. Many of his many books, of which only a fraction had been translated, making them available to me, had dealt with death but not in the sense of our changed relationship to death— like the still-incomparable Philippe Ariès; nor like Canetti, the deadly enemy of death—but, rather, from an esoteric-mythical perspective that saw death merely as a threshold. As a result, his examples were taken from every imaginable religion, and were more magical and incantatory in nature than analytical. During his time as a professor of the History of Religion at Leiden University, he had spent decades poring over the history and arcana of sects with a such passion and excessive zeal that his work had increasingly little to do with academic precision, as his many detractors maintained with great insistence. On the other hand, his books became ever-more attractive to a broader readership. He would have been perfectly happy holding a hundred lectures a year without running out of material or enthusiasm. His knowledge of Hindu and Buddhist sources was intimidating, although he never used it in order to attack others but to convince them, because, in his heart of hearts, I believe, he hoped to be recognized as the head of a secret organization. If I even hinted at something along these lines, he would break out in laughter that was so loud it had already scared off many of his fans and disciples, but I always assumed—or wanted to assume—that he simply wanted to deflect suggestions that threatened to reveal his innermost secrets. The laughter served to create a barrier.

We gathered outside the narrow, seventeenth-century building that was his home. Some of his friends, above all the older ones, were so drunk they could hardly walk. They linked arms and tottered along in ranks of four behind the coffin, which, in turn, followed a Gypsy group that played their tunes at an ear-splitting volume, much to the pleasure of the public who formed a tight phalanx all the way to the town hall. I was amazed by the engagement shown by the whole town as it bade him farewell, although some of the faces bore a look of a silent contentment, clearly stemming from the fact that not all inhabitants of the city of Leiden were sad to see the back of my friend. Too often he had complained about the insufficient generosity of its people, about their self-satisfaction and their political indifference.

There was no talk of this in the speeches at the town hall. If one could understand anything at all, on account of the increasing drunkenness of the speakers, it seemed chiefly to turn on the fact that the deceased had cheated death in his work and, as if to prove the truth of this statement, the coffin, which had been placed on a wooden plinth, began to shift slightly and would have fallen to the floor if a valiant philosopher from Leiden had not prevented it. A carnivalesque mood took hold, reminiscent of the Autumn feast in the Middle Ages. Loud laughter could be heard; some guests left the room to get another drink from the buffet; some others went to sleep. The Brueghel family would have taken great pleasure in the spectacle.

Then the procession set off again. Accompanied by the whole community, it headed for a cemetery outside town; there the solemn, and by now somewhat dissolute, group finally came to the open grave.

The cemetery was a thronging mass of black, like a brittle crust bearing down upon trampled memories. No guest behaved like a guest; people clambered over graves or stood on them to get a better view. No sooner had one's eye adjusted to the swarming black than it began the laborious task of differentiation, of picking out faces: friends and colleagues from the department; authors and other artists whose physiognomy was known to me only from photographs and whom I saw in flesh for the first time; and of course the usual vampires who turn up at such events in order to feed off the aura of the dead.

And then I saw, because it was impossible not to, the fat Cypriot from Venice, the guest from

Room 301, elbowing his way towards the grave, shouting loudly in various languages. He was wearing a sports jacket over a sort of Hawaiian shirt that hung over his trousers. Sweat dripped off his crimson face, and occasionally he held a once-white plastic bag above his head as if it contained something that excused his rude behaviour.

Eventually, he arrived at the grave and stood there, holding the miserable bag in front of his belly, next to the pall-bearer who, still unaware of anything amiss, had just taken off his top hat in order to wipe the sweat from his brow with a red polka-dot handkerchief.

According to the wishes of the deceased, we were now all supposed to file past the open coffin so as to take leave of our friend for the last time. No earth, no flowers, just a final glance.

The dark mass of people seemed reluctant to disband, however, and, because everyone present obviously knew how demoralizing it is to be stuck in line behind a hundred other mourners, one saw the occasional tussle and skirmish until everything settled into something like order. The broad delta of mourners funnelled down, as it were, into the coffin and I really did think that none of them would escape—that my friend would swallow them all. The only one in this snaking queue who had no intention of moving was the Cypriot angel-hunter. Legs akimbo, he stood at the end of the coffin and stared down at the ashen face, as if he were duty-bound to carry out this service. The stream of mourners flowed around him while he, apart from a twitching of his eyebrows, appeared to take no part in procedures.

The closer I was pushed towards the coffin and was able to look at the dead man, the more clearly I saw how much he had shrunk since I last saw him. He looked out from the starched collar of his tailor-made shirt like a dead mouse. The once-aquiline nose had sunk to one side and from his open mouth a tongue the size of a Euro coin protruded. His hands, too, folded over the good-quality cloth, looked like the hands of a newborn. Only the fingernails had kept their original size and, protruding from the tiny nail beds, looked like enormous rat claws.

I allowed myself to be pushed to the side by the mass of mourners so that I could take a longer look at this transformation, but there was no doubt that something inexplicable was happening, something beyond any rational explanation. The smaller our friend's body became, the brighter the face of our Cypriot shone. He seemed to be taking pleasure in this gradual disappearance—I even saw a smile play across his lips. It was wiped away, however, when he lifted his head and saw how many mourners still stood in the queue of people waiting to expunge our friend with their glances.

When he saw me, a lightning bolt of horror shot through his massive body—he pulled himself together and stood up straight in an attempt to resist the obvious thwarting of his plans. Then stared at me with such enmity that I wanted to turn and flee in the opposite direction.

And then came the moment in which there was only the coffin between me and the Cypriot, and inside the coffin the mouse face.

Without exchanging a word of recognition or greeting, we stood opposite each other for long, tortuous seconds, until our angel-hunter suddenly bent down, plucked the head of our friend from his shirt collar, stowed it in his plastic bag and disappeared between the gravestones with a speed of which I would never have thought him capable.

The whole thing happened so quickly that even the pall-bearers, who were now supposed to get on with the job of burying our friend, took a few moments to understand that the corpse no longer had a head. One of them—the one now condemned to die—even lifted the collar to look for it but revealed only a bloody neck no bigger than a thumb. They looked at each other in confusion, then screwed the lid shut and lowered it into the earth.

I was meant to give a speech in honour of my friend at the wake but I couldn't find the paper in one of the many pockets of my suit, nor did I much feel like making an appearance. I passed the people, now happy again, on my way to the exit, found a taxi and asked to be driven straight to the airport.

AN IMPOSSIBLE MARRIAGE

One weekend in May 1967 or 1969, my friend Xaver, a writer, travelled to his sister's wedding in Berlin. Before the journey, as was his way, he had set out in detail, as if he were narrating a chapter from a novel, all the advantages and disadvantages of this union. What interested him was that both families had something against this marriage, not because the circumstances of the other party were too modest but because each was of the opinion— and here, for him, was the rub—that their child was not mature enough to contemplate a partnership intended to last a lifetime. However, because neither family was capable of making this devastating state of affairs clear to their children— although, as Xaver put it, the world and his wife knew the truth—they used whatever means they could to blacken their child's reputation. And they had been, if one was to believe Xaver, largely successful: within the narrow confines of their social milieu, the pair became the subject of ridicule. But

as if providing proof of their own immaturity—
and here Xaver saw the material for an especially
exciting chapter in his novel—the pair refused to
acknowledge the gossip, untruths and welter of
insults directed at them. They neither complained
nor protested, almost as if they agreed with all the
abuse.

Xaver's sister worked in the film service of the
Prussian Cultural Heritage Foundation. On some
days, as he explained in disbelief—she was his
favourite—she had up to two hundred images in
her hands; or, more precisely, two hundred images
passed through her hands, a fact that Xaver felt
was chiefly responsible for her 'occasional limitations'. His sister did not have the pictures in her
hands simply to record their identification number
before they were sent out, but also in order to
make a firm mental note of the objects depicted.
Anyone with that number of objects stored in their
memory—and in a systematic way, not just willy-
nilly—would certainly be immune to the chal-
lenges of the quotidian. Irony, cynicism, any kind
of provocation simply slid off her. Such particu-
larities of human exchange did not fit in any of the
drawers in a brain that managed to store, simul-
taneously and without trouble, thousands of pages
containing the worst sort of invective from the last
two hundred years. She registered the world only
as a series of images; everything else managed to
find a place only by accident.

She met her fiancé in precisely this way—only by accident. He was the picture editor of a daily newspaper with whom she had exchanged hundreds of formal letters without once asking herself who was behind the strange signature. She had not exchanged more than a dozen letters with anyone else in her life, as she felt no inclination to contribute to the growing habit of self-revelation in the world. Moreover, she was discreet. Her discretion went so far that once, having witnessed a bank robbery, she was not prepared to provide—and nor in truth would she have been able to—the physiognomic details of the bank robber, even though she had stood right next to him as he calmly packed the money into a plastic bag. This woman, who carried in her head the tiniest detail of some inconsequential drawing from the eighteenth century, was not capable of describing the man, even in broad outline, who had just, as matter-of-factly as you like, stolen more money than she would earn in ten years. She had not looked at him, Xaver maintained, out of tact. One does not look when somebody has a large amount of money in their hands, especially if one does not know them.

Only once in her long career had she put the wrong picture in an envelope that a courier was waiting to take urgently to a newspaper. A tragedy. The newspaper appeared without a picture, and, even though not a single reader had made a peep of complaint, the editor-in-chief had written a memo to the head of the arts pages warning that, in future, the newspaper should make it a point, when reviewing important exhibitions, of including an impressive image. The head of the feuilleton passed the memo on to the picture editor with a note to the effect that, unfortunately, he was not able to explain why the ordered image did not arrive. And the picture editor sent the memo on to Xaver's sister with a further handwritten note, asking: what is to be done? Xaver's sister soon realized she would have to break out of the circle of formal letters and write a letter of apology to the highly respected picture editor. His answer was so charming and so compelling that a short time later, and against the will of both families, the engagement was announced.

And so Xaver was going to his beloved sister's wedding in Berlin. He wanted to do everything he could to protect her from the family. Above all, the two other sisters had to be prevented from turning the advent of married life—whatever that might mean—into a nightmare. The older sister of his favourite was married to a Scottish pop star, a self-styled genius, responsible for introducing bagpipes into pop music. Because all the musicians were aware that the slow bagpipes would not surrender without a struggle to the new music, the three Scotsmen—who, with the sister's husband, formed a band—applied force, with the result that no one understood anything very much. At least, on the records Xaver brought with him, one could only hear a a loud undifferentiated carpet of sound, or, more exactly, an orgy of bagpipes. These Scotsmen, according to Xaver, had the unpleasant habit of wanting to play at all family events, for free, which meant of course that they had to play. And so, according to Xaver, these scruffy Scots in their little skirts sat there and blew into their bagpipes like mad things until you didn't know whether you were coming or going; and, if anyone complained about this mockery of music, they were given a thorough dressing-down by the uncouth bastards. The only good thing about these bagpipers was that you couldn't understand them. Xaver's sister couldn't understand her own husband either. He had to translate his nonsense into English first, and, if anyone else close by heard him, he would add that the gist of what he had wanted to say had got lost in translation. Of course this band—as Xaver was keen to tell us whenever talk turned to these rowdy crew—was world famous. They had bookings for the next three years and got into hot water with their agent if they wanted to take a day off to drive mad the guests at Xaver's sister's wedding. The sister who was married to one of the bagpipes had got so used to the formless noise that she thought of it— along with her life on the road—as the only pos- sible, that is, alternative, art form, superior to all others. The bagpipe was art itself and the history of the bagpipe was the history of music and culture per se; life on the road was the constant transcendence of barriers and so on. This older sister took every opportunity to go on like this at her family, which is why Xaver was afraid that the bride would get confused and call off the wedding before it was concluded.

The younger sister, too, posed a real and present danger. She was carving out a miserable existence as a Marxist. She had already applied the broad brush of her Marxist convictions to three or four areas of study and now—God knows why—had got German Studies by the throat and was trying to revolutionize it from bottom up. One of her ideologically no-less-unsound habits was to collect shoes. She hoarded hundreds of pairs which stood, in all their rainbow colours, next to the austere blue and brown editions of Marx and Engels and Lenin, Stalin, Trotsky and Ulbricht. The shoes bore witness to a continuing culture of craftsmanship which seemed curiously at odds with the efforts to make the world a better place. It was as if the Marxist heroes had at some point simply given up the ghost. Xaver often shook his head at the universal key of Marxism with which his sister was trying to codify the world. And because she had this shoe-fetish as well, she scoured world literature for any mention of shoes: the walking boots of song or described down to the last detail in prose; the silk shoes peeping out under courtly robes of the eighteenth-century courtesans; the boots of the bourgeoisie and the military. She had a whole card index. And now she was researching how much a royal shoemaker made per hour in Württemberg for crafting three pairs of first-class leather boots, and why that wasn't enough to send his six (surviving) children to the Latin school. These were the kinds of question she addressed in her dissertation. Because she was bossy and argumentative and could not stand a lack of interest in the role of shoes in the class struggle, family gatherings tended to disintegrate into a fight shortly after they had begun, and it was above all the middle sister, the one about to enter into her first marriage, who had to put up with a barrage of Marxist insults because she refused to examine the pictures that went through her hands for signs of class struggle and footwear. She didn't want to talk about it. Because if anyone would have been able to establish an iconography of these two categories, it was her: from fine Greek sandals through to the peasant's thigh boot, she had everything in her mind's eye that had ever appeared in an image.

Xaver, who always worked himself up into a lather when talking about his family, flew into a blind rage while describing his sisters that was only made bearable by his insistence on their comical, bizarre and crazy natures. Because they were crazy they had a secret. And in order to get to the bottom of it, it was necessary to go into great detail. For this reason, when he talked about them, he always started with a description of their faces: the pointed chin of one and the more rounded of the other; the shape of their eyes; how they blew their noses (and what with) and combed their hair; which pullovers they preferred and which skirts; which dresses and why. Once he had got started, he could talk about his sisters for hours. Friends would often egg him on, because, at the end of all the excitement, like an Amen in church, he would come up with a judgement unbeatable in its scorn and malice: his sisters were—apart from the middle one—stupidity made flesh.

These negative attributions also dissuaded me from accompanying him, as he had proposed, to the wedding. For me, the women only existed in his stories, and the idea of coming face-to-face with them, knowing what I did, was less than pleasant. Sometimes I found it quite impossible to think of those women as Xaver's sisters, just as it was sometimes impossible for me to imagine them as sisters at all. Sometimes I even had the impression that he talked about his sisters in the way he might talk about his children. Naturally, they were all the product of the same background that had given rise to Xaver, but I could scarcely imagine, for example, the sisters playing with Xaver as children, or with the other brothers, of whom, conspicuously little was said. It was only the passion that characterized both Xaver and the wayward sisters that hinted at a common family bond, although Xaver's passion could also tip over into such inconsolable and hopeless sadness that one always hoped that it was only his own psyche that was subject to such burdens.

For good reason, my friend Xaver, the writer, gave up trying to write a novel about his family, and, when he reached the point of accepting this defeat, lost not only any interest in writing but also in his family. He became a happy person—a writer no longer driven to write.

*

Now and again I would pick up the writer from the doctor so that he would not have to venture home alone. Out on the street, in the pouring rain, he told me once that after seeing the doctor he would sometimes simply sit in the waiting room until closing time—along with those battered by life on the outside and ravaged on the inside, who saw him, naturally, as competition—because he did not trust himself to be on the street alone. After these injections, he shouted, the world looks so different, it takes a while to get used to it. There had been a summer shower, a sudden downpour that had gone over into continuous rainfall; the passing drivers, who had not reduced their speed despite the rain, sent up great waves of water over our feet as we crossed the main road, the artery between the suburbs and the city, and so we arrived at the writer's house soaking wet. We undressed on the covered terrace, down to our underpants, no longer young men who had just got to know each other over several bottles of white wine, and it was on this occasion that Xaver gave me an overview of his illness, not casually, in passing, but with great concentration, 'Just a quick overview so that you don't feel sick.' If he was to be believed, I was sitting opposite a bag of bones, an empty shell in which the few remaining innards were being tapped or artificially supported or only functioning because of technical assistance, and, in order to underline these grim descriptions Xaver pointed to the wide scars that covered his body from head to toe like rivers, or the hairless parts of his thighs from where they had taken skin for grafts. 'There is a certain moment,' Xaver said, 'when the illness takes over your life. Until that point, everyone is oriented towards a notion of health—nutrition, movement, getting enough sleep—but then the illness takes over and you have your hands full just trying to keep up. Once the illness has broadened out into various illnesses, you can no longer get an overview, marshal it, deal with it. Its attacks are enough to drive you to despair. For example, I have arthritis in my upper thigh, which means that

I can't walk properly and my hips wear down unequally, which in turn means that there is a painful strain in my leg that I can only deal with by taking too many painkillers and sleeping tablets, which in turn means that half my stomach—the other half was removed long ago—has been destroyed, et cetera. Of course, there are things that make it better. When you come to visit me next time, I will show you my collection of medications. But there is no single cure any more.'

'The cure', he said, 'is called death.'

That afternoon we arranged that I would pick up the writer—who was no longer a writer, even though his illnesses forced him to be a storyteller from time to time—from the doctor whenever he had to have a particularly large injection. We'd make long detours home through the English Gardens, sit on a bench for a while or lie on the grass. Sometimes we walked over to the Aumeister beerhall and drank a beer under the chestnut trees while he offered a running commentary on the state of his illnesses: on his bladder, which was beginning to dribble; on the dubious state of his gallbladder, which looked as though it was going to need surgery before long; on circulation problems in his arms and numbness in his left toes; on problems with his vision and back, dizziness and unimaginable pains in his lower jaw, bouts of diarrhoea and heart arrhythmia.

'Why aren't there any magazine for illnesses?' Xaver asked, '*My Illness and Me, All My Illnesses*?' He didn't expect an answer—thank God, because whenever he embarked on one of his long mono-logues it was so liberally punctuated with ques-tions that our conversation would have threatened to expand into a dialogue. But the writer was the only one to talk; I, in contrast, limited myself to few words. And once we had talked about his declining body, he spoke briefly about his earlier successes. Apparently the whole world had lain at his feet. In Germany at least, every school child knew his name and the photo that had been taken of him on his fortieth birthday became an icon. 'An icon!' said Xaver as we sat on a bench in the English Gardens and stared into a green thicket opposite. 'There was a time when I couldn't even cross the road because of the crowds of autograph-hunters ambushing me halfway. It was terrible and wonderful at the same time, a pleasant nightmare,' he muttered, as the sun threatened to disappear behind a row of beech trees.

'Beeches are the trees of shame,' he said, with-out explaining why, and somehow it was true.

*

At the beginning of June, on one of those red-letter days that one notes in the calendar, the writer who was no longer driven to write joined me on my balcony so that we could discuss our summer travels. His Scottish sister had hired a villa on a Greek island for the whole family, where the bagpipes wanted to relax. No music! No social duties! No need to talk! As there had never, in all the years I'd known him, been an occasion on which our holidays had worked out precisely how we had planned them, and because Xaver had reached a level of stability as regards his illnesses, I had two options: either the whole thing would be cancelled at the last moment, as usual, and I would spend the summer on my balcony translating an English novel to keep my head above water; or, if it should actually happen this time, I would have to take six weeks off and then work like a Trojan in the autumn. I watched a tiny bird, which, as I once read and shall never forget, was decorating the cool early morning air with its curlicues of song—and agreed. The thought that I would be able to take a break from the Victorian characters with their tea parties, cake competitions and horse racing, from the erotic allure and boring confessions that I had to translate word for word, was too tempting. It was a world with any number of ingenious crimes and imbroglios but no surprises. Every sentence spoken in the ivy-covered houses was predictable and even the mice, waiting in the dark ivy for someone to open the window so that they could slip inside without hindrance, had their precisely determined role. The scream of the young woman, who was in love with a married nobleman from the neighbourhood, on seeing the mice, would be heard by a stable boy and would furnish proof that she had been in the house at that moment and not in the arms of the nobleman pining for her next door, were it not for the fact that he was busy planning of the perfect crime to get rid of his wife.

The bird that was decorating the cool morning air with its curlicue of song was still busy at its work when Xaver left to start the preparations for the journey. I knew what would happen with the preparations. Xaver was not able to spend even one day without his collection of journals, a veritable library of notebooks, jotters, ring binders and writing pads. Since he had given up on the novels, he circled this accumulation of notes like a sheepdog circling its sheep; these notes, he maintained, in his strange language that tended towards exaggeration, would one day—the day he was preparing for but may not live to experience—make the library holdings of the world superfluous. How exactly that was to happen he did not reveal, of course. 'Wait and see,' he would say cheerfully, if one can use this word to describe his sad, sheeplike face with its teary eyes. 'My day will come.'

Xaver's age was as indeterminate as his background, but when one took a look at the rows of notebooks filled with his tiny handwriting, one could see that he must have been working on them for decades. Sometimes he mentioned this or that philosopher with whom he had studied, which suggested that he must have been to university in several different cities and studied for a long time. A small inheritance had obviously allowed him to live the life of a private scholar and the projected novel about his three sisters was designed to bring him greater acknowledgement. In fact, he had never published anything. No essay, no review, no commentary, however small: nothing that justified the title of writer. His parents, who lived in Baden, occasionally provided him with clean clothes and notebooks on his birthday, and, as he confided one day, were determined to put off death until their beloved child had received due public recognition.

All the journeys we planned came to nothing in the end because it had proved impossible to pack up his handwritten library, even if I offered to take some in my luggage for I always travelled light. And so I prepared myself to spend the summer practising the song of the bird.

*

On 14th July, France's national holiday—a 'day of shame' according to Xaver—we finally arrived on the island, having survived the farce of our overweight baggage and despite all the bother.

They had given us a huge, old rundown house, the biggest house in the village. We had been allocated two neighbouring rooms on the first floor, under the roof, which were impossibly stuffy. But along with the bed and wardrobe was a sturdy table on which, if I felt like it, I could work. I had decided that I would take my translation with me as well as a few dictionaries. While Xaver unpacked his library in the next room, I attempted to exterminate the flies, midges and beetles that had moved in expecting a quiet summer. I went round with a towel, as if possessed, killing anything that moved, until the walls looked as though they had freckles and the floor beneath my feet looked as though it was alive. There was a bedraggled tamarisk tree outside the window, in which honey-coloured birds were busy and in the distance one could see the green waves of the ocean.

Before Xaver and I could visit the only restaurant in the village, I wanted to go down to the sea and dip my hand in the water. The night before, an enormous thunderstorm had broken right over the island so that I could hardly get down the steep path to the beach. The donkeys were overjoyed by the rain which had formed a small pool in the trench behind the sand dune: their usually melancholy faces and hooded, ancient eyes looked bright and enthusiastic. They wanted to make the most of the few hours before they had to start carrying tourists to the Acropolis in the neighbouring village. One of them was rolling in the dark puddle, braying with pleasure through its stumpy brown teeth, and calling so loudly that the others all joined in and, before too long, there was an ear-splitting cacophony that even the bagpipes could never have matched. This heart-rending cry of pleasure, an ecstatic kind of sublimity, held me entirely in its thrall. The whole madness of our existence, the sheer arbitrariness of life that meant that I was there on 14 July, of all days, to witness this rain ritual that was more powerful and more penetrating than the ecstasy described so inadequately in the lifetime of novels I had read and which I had, to some extent, translated from one feeble language into my own. The whole thing made me buckle and left me crouching on the ground, trembling; it wouldn't have taken much for me to lie down with the donkeys in order, just once in my life, to experience such an all-consuming eruption of total abandon. Without knowing what was happening, I had been drawn into the thick of an experience that put all the experiences I could remember, and which made me what I am, into the shade. I stared at the lighter underside of the creature rolling round before me, wet sand dripping from his rounded belly onto his black penis as erect as a telescope; I stared at his hooves which were quite dainty, and his furry ears flicking what was left of the water out of the now-almost-empty puddle.

As if by some secret agreement, everything was suddenly over. The donkey God—I remembered the graffito in the catacombs in Rome that showed Christ with the head of a donkey—had been appeased; and with an unspeakable effort, as if all the gravity of the day rested in their grey coats, the beasts struggled to their feet and stared ahead, just as they had before; motionless, deeply sad, dirty and exhausted with life. For a few minutes they had showed what was hidden in them; now they were back to being beasts of burden.

Down at the shore I met two people who asked for help. One was a fisherman I knew already because he had helped us unload the taxi. Xaver had not lifted a finger: neither when it came to paying which was left up to me, nor when it came to transporting the wardrobe-sized suitcases containing his library up to the top floor. He had simply called out 'Careful!' when the fisherman, without visible effort, had heaved the monsters onto his back. The other was an Italian painter, Piero, who busied himself painting the sea, though no della Francesca. Once as I was complimenting his beautiful house with its studio, Xaver's Scottish sister hissed to me behind her hand that he was tuppence short of a shilling. Since I stopped short, not expecting her to say that sort of thing, she told me the story of his wife: a tall blonde woman from Florence, rumoured to have had a relationship with a fisherman but who, a few days after the rumour started, was found dead in the sea. Of course Piero, the jealous Italian, came under suspicion, but after two days he was back from the city and in his house, painting.

The two of them asked me to help turn over their boat which was now full of water. Piero cast his nets a hundred metres from the shore to catch octopus, and in one of his nets he caught his wife. The sea had been fished out years ago, and in the restaurant the tourists were served Finnish fish from the deep freeze. Only those who had a good relationship with the fishermen were allowed to buy, at exorbitant prices, the little red mullet whose skin turned transparent on the barbecue and splintered in the mouth. Sometimes an octopus.

Piero was rich, that was what one heard about him in the village. His watercolours, pictures built up of many layers of colour, had just been showed very successfully in a big retrospective in America and now he was worried that the worldwide demonstrations against capitalism might bring about a mood hostile to art in the Western world. We sat on his upturned boat and looked at the sea, into which, as if as a sign, the sun sank. Apart from the gentle sound of the waves slipping warily over the stones nothing could be heard; not even the seagulls could be bothered to make the usual din.

Piero must have assumed I was familiar with his work because he confided in me as if I were an expert on the hundred different blues he had mixed in his lifetime, themselves only the tip of the iceberg, because of course there were many more blues to be found. I had the impression that he was not so much a painter as a scientist, who, if he was lucky, would create the perfect blue, one that would rise up out of the ocean of colours, though not with the one-dimensional banality of Yves Klein, whom he described as a juggler, albeit a well-tempered one. He wanted to find a blue with no significance, not pure, of course, but which would reveal itself only once in a lifetime; if you did not pay attention, if you did not, as he put it, keep the window open so that it could come in, then you would have spent your whole life painting for nothing.

All that could now be seen of the sun was a tiny crown that cast a thin strip of sunlight across the water like a narrow jetty; as if he had something vital to tell me, Piero announced into this silence that he came down to the sea every evening at this hour, because it was only in this second, as the sun finally dipped from view, that his wife might appear on this jetty and return to him. At that moment, as if by magic, the strip of light vanished; and I would not have been surprised if this small, wiry man who had just been talking about his successes in New York and Paris and even in Milan, with his flowery American shorts and his elegant shirt open to the waist, had run into the sea, never to be seen again. But he obviously no longer even had any interest in his nets.

In the evening, all the outsiders met on the terrace of the guest house in the village. Xaver too was sitting at one of the scrubbed tables, feeding the thawed fish in front of him to a rather unprepossessing cat which sat on the chair that had been reserved for us, its mouth gaping like a baby bird. 'At last,' he called, 'we literary folk are outnumbered—we need every support!' I squeezed between him and his Scottish sister, eye to eye with the electronic insect repeller that crackled without interruption while around me I could hear the hubbub of chatter about racial unrest, heart transplants and starvation in Biafra. And on my legs I could feel the aggrieved cat, intent on reminding me to whom the lamb cutlet, put in front of me with such lack of finesse, actually belonged. I cut off a large piece and chucked it under the table where suddenly a great caterwauling of multiple cats broke out that was maintained for the rest of the evening.

Opposite us sat a French married couple; he tall and thin with protruding ears, she a pale beauty in a linen dress, a flower behind her right ear and unable to restrain her passion for smoking even during the meal. She had up to three cigarettes on the go at any one time. She lit one, inhaled, laid it down on the scarred table top and forgot all about it. As she gazed dreamily through the smoke of each newly lit cigarette, I secretly poured a few drops of my Ouzo onto the discarded butts; on the one hand, this prevented a fire, but it also caused a mess that had to be cleared away every half hour by the stocky Greek waitress. The Frenchman was busy asking Xaver which French philosophers he knew, but never waited for an answer; instead, he began to name all the French philosophers one should have read. 'Goodness,' Xaver said, which I knew meant that he had read them all or knew precisely why he never intended to, but showed no emotion. The light from the kitchen shone red through the ears of the Frenchman who had modestly placed himself at the end of a long series of his native thinkers, and I was so immersed in that moment that I noticed too late how his beautiful pale wife slipped off her seat and, with a rattle, disappeared among the cats.

I used the commotion caused by the revival of this pale drunken woman to silently slip away, because the village was waiting for me; the village with its sweet-smelling fig trees and the blue television screens behind which men in vests were sitting at tables while women in black sat at the stove; the village with its stray dogs and the cats which disappeared like lightning and whose eyes lit up briefly in the darkness; the village with its raucous Greek music and its smell of burning oil and the occasional call of the night birds. I sat down in the car park on a crumbling wall and stared into the sky; after I counted ten shooting stars and didn't know what else I could wish for, I slid down the wall to the ground, laid my head on my knees and went to sleep.

I was walking on a street as straight as a die and lined with plane trees. It was a beautiful day. I was pulling a handcart behind me, packed with vegetables; on top were leeks, hanging over the side and in danger of falling off. 'This is my work,' I said to myself, 'this cart with vegetables is my work, I will pull it along behind me until I reach the end of the road.' From the end of the street, just visible in the distance, a small dot was moving towards me which suddenly turned into a dog that now stood panting in front of me. Then it jumped onto the cart and began to root around wildly among the vegetables which landed one by one on the street; the cabbage and the leeks, the carrots and the cauliflower, all forming a colourful circle around the cart in which only a few lettuce leaves remained. The dog had clearly not found what it was looking for and leapt onto my back in a single bound with such force that I stumbled and fell. There it lay, on top of me, and bit me repeatedly in the throat while pushing my head down onto the cobbled street with his right paw. I saw how it bit again and again, saw its bloody teeth and felt the boiling blood pumping out of my throat.

From time to time my dreams remind me that I am still alive, although seldom this drastically. In front of me, in the narrow strip between the parked cars and the wall, lay a yellow dog which had been woken by my anguished cry. It shook himself and got to his feet like an old man, stared glumly at the figure leaning against the wall and toddled off. I no longer knew why I was here; nor was I entirely sure who I was. For this reason, I tried to call the dog but it didn't seem to remember me or didn't want to. It didn't turn back and soon vanished between the cars.

I went back to our house, cautiously, like someone who doesn't want to be recognized. Something had broken inside me at the sight of the bloody jowls of the dog, its teeth and tongue that twitched and lapped at the wound at my throat. I wanted to get away from this island as soon as possible, from these people, with whom I—and this was clear to me after my night-time walk through the village—had nothing in common and wanted nothing either: not the French philosopher, not Piero, not the Scottish musicians, nor Xaver's sister. Even the thought of Xaver making friends with all and sundry and sharing his bon mots left, right and centre did not make me happy. The only person who had interested me during this long day was the pale wife of the philosopher, and she had disappeared just like that from our midst. Just as I was thinking of her, I passed a house in which a light was still burning and I looked in at the window, quite shamelessly, like someone to whom nothing more can happen because all possible misfortune has already befallen him. I saw the French philosopher, stripped to his underpants, kneeling by the bed in which the pale woman lay as if dead. Her body was covered by a thin sheet, pulled up to her throat, her sharp nose pointed to the sky. The man's shadow fell on the sheet and trembled slightly while the man himself appeared quite motionless, a beautiful image.

There was a lot of commotion in the kitchen at our house. Everyone was sitting round the big table, bottles and glasses in front of them, torn chunks of white bread and thick wedges of cheese. As they spoke they leapt wildly between four different languages because nobody wanted to listen. A new guest had joined them, an Englishman just arrived from the Himalayas, wanting to try out his Hindu sayings: 'The self does not exist,' he shouted, 'it is simply a mask for Western man who needs reasons as justification.' 'Justification for what?' I heard Xaver shout in English and then the same again, because it was so beautiful: 'Justification for what?' Xaver was lying in wait and soon would show the English simpleton exactly what Western philosophy was. He was biding his time, wanting to lure him out some more before he struck. So the self is just an illusion, is it? That was how he would start, but the Englishman had already turned away. Life with other people is one endless distraction, you can't do anything about that.

I stood at the sink and drank some water. A tiny green beetle had attached itself to the glass. Hopefully it doesn't understand anything, I thought, and went to bed.

*

By morning the sea was completely calm and appeared to be asleep. If you looked long enough, you could see how it breathed as if it was trying to keep itself in check. I walked very slowly, as if on tiptoe, into the water, and, when it reached my hips, I let myself slide in. I tried desperately to think about something that was not to do with water. I thought about Xaver, the writer who was no longer driven to write, and about his three sisters, particularly the middle one, who had all those pictures in her head because she couldn't forget anything.

The sun stood high in the sky, obscured only occasionally by clouds whose shadows wandered across the surface of the sea; yes, wander, that's the right expression. When I turned over onto my back to relax, the island had disappeared.

At last, I shouted into the endless sky, you are on the right side.

POST

For some time now I have been receiving letters that, if they continue to arrive, will turn me into someone else. The envelopes are addressed to me. My name and address are written correctly, and generally in a hand that looks as though somebody of dubious character has taken pains to imitate my own. In the last few years I have tried to bring a certain calligraphic flourish to my writing: for instance, I add such a long tail to my lowercase 'f' that it couldn't really be described as a descender any more. In fact, each letter has over time taken on a quite particular form, that has, moreover, also continued to evolve, so that I would be able to use comparative analysis to establish at what point the correspondent had taken on my identity (and my writing style). But what would be the point of that?

The first issue is that the letters themselves are not addressed to me but to seven people (all male so far) with the following names: Franz, Gerhard, Otto, Wilhelm, Martin, Dieter and Johannes. Everyone in my part of the world, and evidently that of my correspondent, knows men who answer to such names, but none of my friends or relatives have had to go through life with one of these run-of-the-mill monikers. Dear Franz—I have nineteen letters that start with this greeting. Of course I have asked myself as I read whether the content determines the choice of forename, i.e. whether there are specific Dieter-letters that are essentially different from the Otto-letters?

Is the correspondent trying to make me understand that I, like everyone else, am made up of many characters and identities, but that they can all be measured by the same yardstick? I don't know.

My friends have advised me to open letters addressed to me but not to read them if the greeting should contain a name different to my own. They mean well, I'm sure, but in practice this is not so easy, because the letters arrive in envelopes addressed to me, talk exclusively about me and with such an eye for detail and with such extremely precise knowledge about my personality and my activities, views and convictions, that I cannot help devouring them avidly in the hope of finding my name on the last page, because no one, no wife, no psychiatrist, no fellow sports fan, no colleague could know as much about me, apart from myself. But none of the letters is signed, either by me or anyone else.

Nevertheless, I have to come to terms with the fact that only I can be the correspondent.

MY SIX CHILDREN

We have observed our children frequently and carefully. There were moments when they were close to us and others when we had to take a long hard look before things came into focus. Occasionally, we took refuge in the perhaps somewhat pedantic fact that we had parents of our own who were also present in our children, although my wife was increasingly less inclined to accept that. Rising panic, secrecy, a sense of mission: these could be blamed on me because her family had allegedly been free of any such traits for generations. So we watched our children grow up without, strictly speaking, ever being allowed to get to know them. The children were grateful for this for a long time. They took part in our life without really disturbing it.

For some time now, changes have been taking place that give grounds for concern. Our six children—this is the devastating conclusion of my conscientious observations over the last months— are tending in directions completely alien to us. All six, the one-syllable boys (Fritz, Franz and Max) as well as the two-syllable girls (Anna, Hannah and Ulla), have told us in no uncertain terms that they want to live the rest of their lives without what my wife and I would understand as 'culture'. At first I was inclined to treat this as a fad, as an understandable reaction to a family home saturated with culture, where the library and the grand piano take centre stage. But when even our youngest, Max—who had undertaken a successful apprenticeship as a bookseller with a publisher—gave up looking at the cultural pages of the newspaper for the economic section, when he openly declared that books no longer had, for him, any aesthetic value and that he was only interested in their market value; and since, more-over, he started talking about literature exclusively in terms of market saturation, I realized I had to give up on him as well.

We saw the signs first in Anna. She was an enthusiastic worshipper of Pina Bausch's so-called dance-theatre. How often she had skipped school in order to hitchhike to Vienna, Wuppertal or Essen where the latest productions were being staged, and how often she had defended dance-theatre against conventional theatre of the sort we tended to frequent, from *Hamlet* to *Horvath*. How cynically she had laughed when her sister Hannah enthused at breakfast about the new *Tasso*, which we, my wife and I, had left during the interval. And Hannah, who shared a room with Anna, made us promise to let her move in with Ulla because all the talk about dance-theatre was ruining her nerves; while Anna, pleased to have more room for herself, began, straight out of school, to copy the crude moves of so-called dance-theatre, which led to considerable disruption of domestic peace. But the frenetic interest in dance-theatre has lessened in the last few months; and since she started her studies in economic and cultural management, she has only ever spoken about dance-theatre in the past tense.

My wife is of the opinion that we must assume that our daughter's love of dance-theatre has completely burnt out. At first I was happy about this news, because the constant twitching and throwing herself to the ground, the uncontrolled screaming, even among strangers on the U-Bahn, for example, had made me concerned that our Anna would be completely taken over by this strange hybrid genre. But when I glimpse her now, sitting silently in her fashionable suit, brooding over the business plans for her course in cultural management, I find myself longing for the wild times again. In any case, today she manages to get by without any culture at all and has also taken pains to reassure me that cultural managers, by definition, consider it inappropriate to come into direct contact with culture. She agrees with Max on this point. Both of them work intermittently on a beautiful plan to one day open a cultural-project management agency that they will float on the stock market in the third year, and then spend the rest of their days on an island in the Mediterranean. Three hundred poets to Erfurt. A choral competition in Sulzbach. The body/culture Biennale in Tübingen. My wife, who identifies wholeheartedly with the old sense of culture, is alarmed by this sort of talk. Why an island? she asked me recently. Why do they want to leave the mainland?

Hannah's love of the theatre, too, has suddenly disappeared. Only yesterday the world consisted exclusively of Tasso, Hamlet, Richard and Lear, of great feelings and pathos and the culture of language, of morality and illusion, entrances and exits, lighting and the avoidance of representation, so that my poor wife feared my daughter would become an actress. The way she walked into a room! The way she giggled about her make-up kit, as if she were Beckett's Winnie, the way she pushed her plate away and brushed the hair from her forehead: all of which pointed to the fact that one day we would have to admire her on stage. Perhaps even naked, my wife muttered, a naked Desdemona! We would probably have to go and live in a different city after my retirement. But for some months now the theatre has been dead: no power to innovate any more, as Hannah puts it. Now she wants to become a life coach and that would mean that her theatre studies could still be of use without her having to be reminded of theatre and dead art. How one presents oneself, sells oneself, makes an impression, how one plays a role convincingly. She now intends to study Human Resource Management, a subject with a future. Although my wife can still not quite imagine what exactly Hannah would do as a life coach, she is relieved. At least her daughter will remain fully clothed at work.

Ulla, our youngest, was always the problem child. She was introverted, said little, ate little, slept little, but drank a lot. Even cigarettes agreed with her. And she drew. School meant nothing to her. She sat drawing for hours on end. She was attracted to surrealism: entwined with the erotic but always with a dreamlike precision. My wife claimed she could see images of sexual union in some of her colour work, penetration, turned on its head, as it were, but the longer we stared at the pictures the less sure we became. *Becoming and Departing* is my favourite, though we never did discover what it is meant to represent. It simply represents, my daughter said, when we asked her, which my wife described as out-and-out rudeness. Ulla had problems with behaviour but was good at relationships. Last year she was thrown out of school but by May had already found herself a place at the Academy with Professor Karsch who, after looking at her erotic aquarelles, obviously took a shine to her. Carry on like that, was the only thing he'd said to her by the end of November because his exhibitions left him no time for teaching. At the beginning of December, Ulla was allowed to help put together his exhibition in Regensburg; heaps of sand had to be built up into exquisite layers in the corners of the gallery. The sand came from earthquake zones in Peru and, because it had got all lumped together on the journey to Regensburg, now had to be sieved. The Devil's own work but an impressive result. Ulla received thanks in the catalogue. By Christmas, my daughter had left the Academy again. Now she is working as the assistant to an aristocratic lady who runs the firm Art Management which sells art to big firms for their empty walls. She now earns twice as much as I do. My wife is very happy. Our Ulla! She sold the sand that was left over in Regensburg to an engineering company which keeps it away from the inquisitive hands of the tax authorities behind Plexiglas in the corners of their conference rooms. It is extraordinary how business has such a sense of art. And our Ulla is always there and never has to get her hands dirty.

That leaves Fritz and Franz, who also want nothing more to do with culture. Fritz studied philosophy, Franz music. Fritz was the genius of the family. While his schoolmates were reading

Mickey Mouse, he claimed he had read Hegel's *Phenomenology of the Spirit*. Top marks in his A-levels, scholarships from the German National Academic Foundation and German Research Foundation, exchange student at Harvard, reviews in philosophical monthlies. But something was wrong. My wife became suspicious when Fritz used the final pages of his unfinished doctoral thesis—'The End of the Philosophy of History'—as scrap paper. And then one evening he came into the sitting room and explained that, to cap it all, he had failed to take cognizance of the *linguistic turn*. How could that have happened, my wife asked? It was all over. There was, nevertheless, a silver lining. He has been an online lifestyle consultant for the last four weeks. No more theory, just an honest day's work, my wife says, and, besides, he earns three times what a junior professor who had followed the *linguistic turn* would. Day and night he sits in his pyjamas and advises people who comes to his chatroom and say they have lost all direction in life. We hardly see him any longer but the faint clicking of his computer keyboard tells us that he must still be alive. Sometimes we hear him in the night, crying out. We should probably get used to that.

Franz was the very epitome of an artist. Long wavy hair, thin as a matchstick, intense eyes, and always dressed in a black greatcoat. He was awarded the composition prize in Bari for his piece for two pianos and a trumpet, his 'Configurations I-XII' was premiered in Leipzig and then played in Nuremberg. He conducted it himself. In 'Configuration IX', a wind-up duck runs across the skin of the bass drum, which earned him a reputation for gimmickry but he stuck to his guns. He was completely immersed in his art. Music is the only art that makes the incommensurable audible, he said. It will survive us all. Each note is a gift from silence. Franz always had the capacity to amaze us with comments like that. Six weeks ago there came something really incommensurable. Anyone who writes a note, he instructed us at breakfast, should be declared insane. Everything was senseless, everything was codswallop and he had given all his notes their marching orders. And while my wife fought back her tears, unable to speak, Franz left the room, sold his instruments, had his hair cut and purchased an Armani suit and a Rolex. He has taken a job at a private television company, as head of the music department. Head of canned music. As I write this, we are listening to his programme 'Voices of the World', in which a four-year-old with a teddy bear in his arms is singing 'Ave Maria', much to my wife's delight.

We were all together again at Christmas, apart from Fritz, who has a particularly busy time in his chatroom during the festive season. We ate goose.

Afterwards everyone played with their laptops, corresponded with friends, did a little business. Life went on. And to this day we still think frequently and at length about our children.

THE GIRL ON THE STAIRS

It was Sunday, and, as was the way every Sunday, I went to the 'Pfalzstube'. In truth, I visited this pub every day except Saturdays—that was when the footballers were in, and it was best to steer clear of them. The food was generally atrocious since neither the landlord, with whom I had been friends for decades, nor the constantly changing kitchen personnel, knew anything about cooking. When I moved to Munich in my youth, the 'Pfalzstube' was the bohemian meeting place. Writers, film people, artists and, later, also the so-called terrorists would gather in this pub which even then had little to recommend it. It was run by a woman whom everyone called Ma. And when Ma lay dying with lung cancer, she left the pub to her most loyal customer, Kurt, or Kurti as he was known, who was in fact a sculptor. In the summer, Kurti would disappear for three months to his country place in Piedmont to teach women of a certain age how to make sculptures of animals; sheep and rabbits, mostly. The rest of the time he would stand behind the bar, complaining about modern artists who apparently understood nothing about craft. Nevertheless, a few of these artists remained loyal to Kurt. They had become professors of art at the Academy and had large exhibitions, but when they visited Kurt they sat at the bar playing dice and discussing football. Even I was surprised sometimes by how uncommunicative they were, but, when I went to pass comment, Kurt defended them absolutely. Only he was allowed to criticize them—not me, the non-artist. His romantic notion of the artist as creator did not allow one to make jokes about art; and even if the creator had become a star who now only plagiarized himself, he was still an artist who was to be respected. Neither logic nor theory numbered among Kurt's strengths, and any attempt to engage him in a conversation about the significance of art and artists was doomed to fail after a few minutes. Art is handiwork. He had nothing more to say on the subject.

Kurt's great strength was friendship.

The 'Pfalz' was full apart from the table reserved for me, which was unusual because on some Sundays I was the only mealtime guest. It couldn't be the Königsberg dumplings, which the Vietnamese chef, an expert on German specialities,

according to Kurt—generally neither German
nor special—was offering as a main course. The
Vietnamese chef was a trained mathematician
who had lost all his money, along with that of a
number of others, on the horses, and for that
crime had spent eleven months in prison where he
discovered his love of German cuisine. He was, in
contrast to Kurt, an entrepreneurial fellow, and for
this reason we were certain that we would soon
see him as the head of a Vietnamese fast-food
chain.

I ordered the Königsberg dumplings because I
had already forced down everything else on the
menu that week. I didn't know any of the noisy
guests and Kurt shrugged his shoulders too when
I asked him about the sudden popularity of his
food. A tourist bus, was his answer, and indeed I
heard Swabian accents as the crowd shouted for
beer. At home Swabians are a quiet and peaceful
people, Kurt said, but as soon as they leave their
homeland they become wild animals. Kurt came
from Husum, the grey city on the coast, where, as
he said, there hasn't even been a snigger since the
war against Denmark.

I hunkered down at my little table and began
to read the book I had brought with me. It was a
study of nineteenth-century curiosities—mediums,
dwarves and sea monsters—but also Lola Montez
or Jack the Ripper, Siamese twins and Joanna

Southcott who had predicted the exact date of the second coming. It was a strange mixture of epiphanies about the improbable and unpredictable such as only England, in its quirkiness, could produce, and had been published in 1945. Books like this captivated me much more than the contemporary novels I had to proofread. Above all, they were, as a rule, printed without errors; something one could certainly not say about the many novels, or even textbooks, the sloppy manuscripts of which I was sent by various publishers. My reputation as a diligent and reliable copy editor was now so well established that I could pick and choose; accompanying the most interesting projects from the manuscript stage via the galley proofs to final publication. I used to write novels myself and they are still available as e-books, but there was a moment in which I lost all confidence in fiction, in my ability to invent it. Perhaps it's only a hiatus, I used to think, part of a process that develops and then dies off, just as every individual is a process and not static or genetically fixed. Perhaps even back then, something inside me, inside my self, did not want to waste any more time on the inventions that grew out of me, indeed splurged out of me (something praised at the time as great artistic productivity). Maybe this self wanted to experience something and feel itself changed by it: and my role was to document this change in minute detail.

But I was not capable of having a life-changing experience. It was with great pain, agonies indeed—for I had been happy to become a writer—that I had to concede that I was not able to open myself up, to throw open the windows and doors of my being and let the fresh air of the new and different in. The more I worked on trying to even imagine this new, this other, the less I was convinced by the results. I had, I was forced to admit, nothing to offer either the revolution in art (and life) or the wonderful performance culture that brought fresh air into conventional petty-bourgeois art scene in those years.

I remember the performance artist Wolf Vostell, who was famous back then, a heavy man in a long fur coat. One day he sonorously invited me to take part in a 'happening' with him, but I suddenly realized what a ridiculous figure I would cut—and said no. I was not made for that sort of thing; I simply couldn't play the flute on the motorway—for this was the intention—while the rush hour went on around me. The key point was that the flute was to be inaudible. I was to play a shepherd's song—and I was a wonderful flautist back then!—that was to be inaudible while it was clear to me that the wonderful Wolf Vostell should go and stop the traffic so that all of them would be forced to listen to my music! I remember with what growing despair I pleaded with the performance artist to give the flute an audience, while he, with a certain lethargy, insisted that the whole joke was that it wouldn't be heard.

I soon reached the end of my career as a conceptual artist. I rented the shell of a multistorey car park that was under construction and invited twelve artists *not* to exhibit their work there. A cultural forum and a brewery had supported the project with a lot of money and we had put up posters. I had given highly theoretical interviews, so a good crowd turned up for the opening and walked through the empty building carrying their free beer and seeing nothing but themselves. A politician asked why such nonsense should be supported out of the public purse. There were protests and counter-protests, as usual, and I was happy for a few days.

There were many such fiascos in those days. They stemmed from the fact that, on the one hand, I was friends with several artists who frequented the 'Pfalzstube' and were making a name for themselves (and who are all dead now); on the other hand, I myself could not constantly reinvent myself. I wanted to be a proper artist and not just exhibit nothing. So, at some point, I also stopped my writing activity, if you disregard the occasional satire which came easily and which the radio liked to broadcast (and paid well for). But satire has nothing to do with art as I understand it and so I allowed this source of income to dry up and became a proofreader instead, a job in which one learns not only a lot about language and punctuation but also about context.

I was deep into Joanna Southcott's predictions when Kurt asked me if a late guest could join me at my table, an old friend of his who was interested in the last Königsberg dumplings. Without really looking closely I agreed and was then amazed to see the collapsed face of the person who was just about to take his seat opposite me. It was clear that some neural inflammation had paralysed the right side, creating an asymmetry which made normal speaking impossible. Probably Bell's palsy. The right side of his mouth flapped open as he thanked me for my friendliness in not having turned him away. After every word a fleshy tongue passed over his lips, like a sponge wiping away every word the moment it had been uttered. I didn't even understand his name. He folded his light summer coat fastidiously over the back of his chair, sat down with care, repeatedly shifting the chair until it was in an acceptable position. At first I was not sure whether he wanted to talk to me because he maintained his distance, and even seemed hostile, as if I had invaded his territory without permission and not the other way round.

And then, just as Kurt had plonked the last Königsberg dumplings in front of him, he said, with a voice that seemed to come from the deepest depths of his clumsiness, how nice it was to see me again after so long. Is it twenty, twenty-five years, he asked me, since we last saw each other? I was speechless: I could swear that I didn't recognize this face and I prided myself on my ability to recognize a face.

He knew everything about me. Everything. Every leaflet to which I had contributed, every demonstration in which I had participated. He even recounted conversations that I had apparently held with him, not to mention all the failed love affairs that he began to list with uncanny accuracy. The Swabians had left the pub in the meantime and there were just two guys in leather jackets, who I did not recognize, hanging around at the bar, both of whom had placed their elbows on the counter and one foot on the foot rest that ran around it; a fine image of harmonic symmetry. In 1814, Joanna Southcott, I remembered, had predicted that at the end of the year—she was sixty-four years at the time—she would bear a son who would be the second Messiah and whose task it would be to bring reconciliation between Christians and Jews. The poor woman died on 27th December 1814.

Christoph, for that was my search engine's name, drank one beer after another and came up with ever-more details about my rebellious youth, with the result that at the end of this unusually long evening I was sure that we must've known each other once. He was a theologian but had abandoned his doctoral dissertation about the problems of theodicy because he had joined the armed struggle in South America for a few years. 'Venceremos,' came out of his lopsided mouth, you know what I mean, don't you? So you are one of those who have turned away from God, I said, and regretted it straight away because I feared that I would have to hear every last detail about his fall from grace, a chapter of German intellectual history I knew back to front. Please don't! I cried as he was about to start confessing his break with the church, with gobbets of Karl Barth, something that God had not deserved. There is nothing more tedious than earnest Protestants expounding their doubts about God in Bavarian restaurants.

On the other hand, I took great pleasure in this late guest whose life did have similarities to mine when looked at closely. I too did not finish my studies, but not because I had studied too little but rather too much. Every semester I flung open a new window letting every doubt in; I no longer read with care, but devoured books greedily one after another, allowing every new question to take root; at the end of these wonderful years, I even managed to find a reason why it was a mistake to try to direct this broad delta of knowledge, in which I had been swimming happily and without a goal, into the narrow gully of a dissertation. But I didn't wish to burden Christoph with this too.

So I paid, or rather I asked Kurt to put it on the slate (for both of us!), even though I had decided to avoid the 'Pfalz' in the coming weeks in order to avoid Christoph. I sensed that he wanted to get closer to me and I was suddenly afraid that he could know something about me of which I did not, under any circumstances, wish to be reminded. I was, as I am happy to admit, a committed repressor and I didn't want to spend the years that were left to me poking around in old stories. My soul was not pure: I knew that better than anyone. I didn't need a failed theologian to prove it to me.

Christoph walked two paces behind me. Sometimes his shadow lurched ahead and then got shorter and retreated to the next street lamp. There was no doubt he wanted to follow me. But where to? Mrs Southcott was quite certain that she would come to life again four days after her death. And some of her supporters were convinced that she would give birth to the child that would become the Messiah after her death. But God had already taken the child to himself. We went past the house of Carl Werner, the fraudster, whose story I shall write one day. It is no less dramatic than that of poor Mrs Southcott, which I now started relating to Christoph, and when we finally got to my house it seemed quite natural to invite him in for a nightcap. He accepted without hesitation.

*

The house I live in is an old art-nouveau building with a lift that only works once a month. So we climbed up to the third floor, grumbling and with long breaks to catch our breath, during which I related Carl Werner's story, how he succeeded in going from being the son of a baker from Giessing to a leftist radical with the blue blood of the Hohenzollerns in his veins. We all profited from him and his mysterious foundations. I myself had written exposés for urban studies and planned congresses on the future of how we live, and Carl Werner, in whose functional flat trade union bosses and industrialists met with us over the cheapest wine, paid for everything without ever asking any questions. Once I invited the Viennese philosopher Ernst Fischer to a discussion. Carl Werner greeted him as if they were long-lost friends, although Fischer whispered to me that he had never seen the man before in his life. The wife of one philosopher had baked biscuits especially for the occasion; the industrialists were excited about the opportunity to listen to such a prominent communist with such good manners; and the radical drinkers from the 'Pfalz' doughtily partook of the red wine in three-litre bottles. As I spoke, I could see before me the sad face of Wolfgang Koeppen, also a guest of this mad fraudster. He hated bad wine.

It had taken a long time for us to understand that the world could not be changed. It is always a little bit more powerful than we are. And even if seven billion people make the effort to turn it into a scrapheap, it will still survive in the long run. It will simply, God knows how, speed up a little and fling all the people and things off to burn up in space. Then the whole story will start over again, from the beginning. And all the mistakes will be repeated. Carl Werner, the friendly fraudster, knew all this, of course. The director of the Botanical Gardens himself turned Carl's tiny balcony into a sort of jungle in which he, drinking his cheap wine and smoking his cheaper cigarettes, could think about how he could cheat certain people out of money and put it in our pockets. To listen to him, it was quite simple. He had published three volumes of poetry. When he died, it came out that he had made up the story about his noble background. At his funeral, his many friends were nowhere to be seen. Only his brothers and sisters were at his graveside and they told me about their parents' bakery. Naturally, his name was an invention too.

*

Sitting on the steps in front of my flat was a young woman, or, more accurately, a howling ball of misery. Next to her was a suitcase and a gigantic folder, like those used to carry drawings. She had scattered the contents of her handbag on several steps, as if she was intending to live in this hallway for some time. It was quite an image: a woman crying softly but without pause, her trousers deliberately torn at the knees, her coat hanging over the banisters; and around her tablets, combs, books, electronic gadgets, make-up, keys and other strange things that are only familiar to those who, without ever needing them, carry them around their whole lives long.

She was, to put it in a superficial way, very beautiful. And she was not shedding her tears, this was clear to everyone involved in this drama, on account of me.

The three of us made ourselves comfortable in my living room. I removed the mountains of books from all the chairs and Christoph disappeared into the kitchen with the beautiful visitor to cook her some spaghetti; naturally, he generously tipped a whole packet into the boiling water so that he could keep her company while she ate. The rules of hospitality meant that I had no choice but to invite the girl, who had told us her story in the hallway, in. My neighbour, one of those good-looking young men who have been drawn almost magnetically to this part of town of late, had invited her around but wasn't able to look after her properly, because, just as she arrived at the door, the police were taking him away. Probably drugs. He made TV ads, or so he said, drove a Porsche and in general looked as though his life was pretty effortless. His parents, our new friend told us, owned a chain of building suppliers and several hotels in the North. The mother bred racehorses. I had met him fleetingly, and we had exchanged the usual courtesies whenever we handed over any wrongly delivered post or met by chance on the stairs. He was always well-dressed and had an exaggeratedly polite manner and when I once asked him to turn his music down after midnight because I wanted to work, he deluged me with a torrent of apologies. There was a particular type of music that sent him, quite literally, into ecstasy, so he no longer recognized himself, that was the upshot of his apology: it was probably due to the drugs. You could see from looking at him though that he didn't know himself particularly well in any case. The large brass sign on his door said 'Mega-Cine'. Enough said.

The young woman's name was Helga. Christoph, who thought it unlikely that his guest would want to discuss problems of theodicy and that there would probably be no satisfactory answer to the question of why God had taken so long to free the world from suffering, tonight at least, asked her what her name was. Helga, from Hannover. I recoiled. How could parents call their daughter Helga? How could they allow their beautiful daughter to be addressed by the name Helga for the rest of her life? Hardly anyone realizes what damage names can do, how they can destroy a life. More than anything I wanted to stand up, take her into my arms and comfort her; but I held back. Thomas Mann would have remained an unknown provincial writer from Lübeck, I reflected, if he had given one of the characters in his novel the name Helga. A Helga in *Buddenbrooks* would have destroyed the novel.

Helga did not have any money. Someone had stolen her purse on the train from Hannover, 'with all my cards, everything gone', she said, trustingly, and I recalled that among all the things that she had spread out in our hall there was no purse. Our guest was turning into an interesting case.

We decided that Helga would sleep in the guest room which I had hurriedly got ready. Christoph took the last bottle and headed off home and I went to bed with Mrs Southcott. It was strange that even after her death she still had her acolytes. It was thought that if people had treated her better, God would have sent the Messiah to be born to her. 'Humans are only significant and lucid as a puzzle,' a friend of mine once wrote, 'only mystical anthropology can do humankind justice.'

*

My neighbour did not put in an appearance over the next few days but remained in custody, as a policewoman proudly told me on the telephone. Perhaps, though I hadn't credited it, he had indeed been involved in something big. With his friendship bands, his gold chain and open shirt, his silly cowboy boots and diamond earrings, he looked like any one of the wannabes who go about their harmless business in Munich's old quarter. One sees them in the Elizabeth Market just before it closes, buying papaya and rucola and fat-free yoghurt for their late breakfast.

Helga spent a large part of the following days on the telephone, blocking her old cards and ordering new ones. She also applied for jobs as a graphic designer because she had fallen for my neighbour's promises that he would get her a lucrative career and so had given in her notice in Hannover. She had met Per, where else, on Ibiza. Helga and Per, she just liked the sound of it; though the combination turned my stomach. What sort of creature hangs around in Ibiza, never reads a book—as she proudly told me—never listens to music that is more than three months old and then falls for a man called Per? I have never had a high opinion of pedagogy, but what they teach in the schools these days drives me mad. At the same time, Helga was the nicest person you could wish to meet. An angel, who had been sent, of all people, to me. She cleaned things that had resolutely resisted all cleaning before, sorted my books into alphabetical order, repaired the toaster and the vacuum cleaner, was good at shopping and could even make a passable lunchtime meal.

If only she hadn't constantly gone on about calories. Her greatest achievement, however, was to give my entire wardrobe the once over. Torn seams were mended, long-lost buttons sewn on, trousers cleaned and ironed, underpants washed and folded, shoes given new soles and decent laces.

After a few months I began to think that I had changed under Helga's meticulous care. But of course she was only responsible for the external, for the skin of my life. She had a healthy instinct that prevented her from getting close to anything deeper. Sometimes I got the impression that she was scared of me. When we ate together, she would sometimes look at me for a long time without saying anything. And didn't take a bite herself.

After six months, she found a part-time job as a web designer. Per was sentenced, and a couple moved into the flat next door whom I did my best to avoid, even though Helga asked me to invite them around out of neighbourliness. She often went next door. Very nice people, she explained, the woman was a virologist, the man an ear, nose and throat specialist at the city hospital. But I couldn't muster the energy to dedicate an evening to them. The longer I remained under Helga's care, the more I wanted to maintain the illusion that my decisions were my own. I didn't think much of the idea of free will and feared that the medical people next door would drive the last of it out of me. If you are buried all day in ears, noses and throats, you lose any sense of metaphysics, let alone free will; and free will without metaphysics is impossible. As a young man, I had given too much thought to freedom. Everything should be free. Now I knew that there was no such thing as freedom. There was no freedom. When would people understand this simple truth?

One day, Helga sent me into the city to collect a special support for my neck which was stiff because of all my proofreading. How different the city seemed to me! I had not walked round the streets for months, ever since Helga had started keeping me like a voluntary prisoner. For me, she was the city. She went to the cinema and to bars and concerts and told me all about the new building sites and businesses; about organic shops and galleries. She provided more and more details each day and all I needed to do was imagine what was going on outside the four walls of my flat.

To be honest, I also didn't miss the city very much. I had only ever really used the city amenities, as they say, out of a sense of duty as a resident. For example, I had gone in to vote, or do my shopping, as one does, but I can't say that I had really ever taken part in city life. And because I no longer visited the 'Pfalzstube', there was no pressing reason to go out at all. I spent all day reading and was pleased if Helga was home in the evening because I could discuss everything I had read with her. My view of the world wasn't exactly becoming more optimistic, which often led to heated exchanges with Helga who on the whole thought world bearable. For me it was only Helga who made the world bearable.

I also stopped travelling. I used to book city tours occasionally and went to Berlin or Leipzig to see *Hamlet* or to hear Beethoven; but the people who undertook such bus trips were getting older and deafer and less interesting, and the idea of sitting next to a culture-obsessed widow for hours on end driving through Germany to see a badly staged *Hamlet* in Cologne was no longer an attractive prospect. One absorbed far too much mediocre culture and it was difficult to get rid of it again. The ghosts of all the terrible Kasimirs and Karolines I had seen in my life were inside me, blocking everything else; I was over the moon when I read in the newspaper that performances these days weren't a patch on the ones in my youth. Sometimes I really did have the feeling that the world had run out of ideas. Apart from the means of its own destruction. Helga naturally made the occasional effort to whip me off to festivals in Schwetzingen or Heidelberg; and sometimes I even got close to saying yes but at the last moment I always managed to invent some reason to cancel the trip.

I met Kurt at the Elizabeth Market. I almost didn't recognize him, so convivial did this usually unkempt man look, as if someone had torn a mask from his face. He said that Helga had become the life and soul of his pub, and wanted to thank me from the bottom of his heart. From the bottom of his heart. Kurt had probably not used this expression for forty years. From the heart, tears me apart; I muttered the phrase to myself because I suddenly felt a stabbing pain throughout my body.

Something had escaped me, something decisive. Helga left the flat around midday each day and came back around four, and, naturally, I had assumed that she was doing her job as a web designer. No clue what she was really up to. Advertising, was all she said when I asked her. Afterwards she would 'knock the flat back into shape' (her expression), and make the evening meal that would always be on the table by six o'clock. And then she would disappear again. Naturally, I had never asked where she was off to. I had never assumed that she went to the technical college or to the library; but that she had been to the 'Pfalzstube' every night and become the life and soul of the pub, came as a shock. I was happy when she was back around midnight and could listen to my philosophical observations. Although nothing had changed in my life, I suddenly felt very alone. I could hardly move, just stood there, with my neck support under my arm, an old man who had lost his bearings. I was standing next to a stall for the Socialist Party calling for better air quality and couldn't breathe. The comrade, who was wearily handing out leaflets, offered me her stool so that I suddenly became part of a campaign against fine particulates.

I went home and lay down on the sofa with my new neck support but the pains did not go away. On the radio—I had switched it on against my normal habit, to provide a distraction—was a program about theodicy on the cultural station of Radio Bavaria, and, before I could catch my startled breath, I heard Christoph's voice, contemplating why it was that people always gave into the temptation to do evil. Is evil an integral part of our world, he asked himself sanctimoniously, and, of course, responded in the affirmative. So Christoph could speak properly again. His voice still sounded a little choked, as if he had to make an effort, but you could understand him well enough. God does not give up anything for lost, despite the evil in the world, I heard him say, and we can and will be sure of that when we let him into our hearts.

So, he had found his way back, the drunken renegade, and was now discussing theological questions on Radio Bavaria. Is one allowed to think about God and his hidden intentions on Radio Bavaria without at least respecting him?

Helga came home around four, breathless. How beautiful she looked in her breathlessness. When I told her that Christoph had been on the radio talking about God's good memory, she said simply: all the things that man thinks and says, hardly credible. That was all. Not one word about whether she had seen him or how he was. Not one word.

And then, after she had removed the terrible neck brace and massaged me, we had our evening meal. It was gammon steak with sauerkraut. Stewed fruit for afters. While she was clearing away the dishes, Helga asked me whether I would mind if she got a dog. Dogs have something against me, I don't know why: they bark at me, but I have never understood exactly what they want from me. I am nonplussed when they stand yapping at me, opening their mouths as if I had done something to them. When Helga noticed my hesitation, she said that actually she wanted to get the dog for me, because I urgently needed a dog. Only a dog can save you, she said, and at first I thought that it was a humorous response to Christoph's thoughts on theodicy, but she was serious. And so I agreed, and I knew, of course, that the dog had already been acquired and was merely waiting for its entrance.

It suddenly became clear to me that the dog was a way of introducing Helga's departure. 'He could feel the despairing house around him and above him the dying leaves, and how in his soul the one bright, urgent star of joy trembled as it died': these lines from one of my favourite books came into my mind, so I opened it straight away and my eye fell on the words: 'even the value of his own life seemed doubtful to him.' So a dog was being acquired so I would have company and then Helga would go. The age of angels was coming to an end.

I heard Helga shut the door behind her, carefully, as ever, so as not to frighten me, but I was frightened down to the depths of my soul.

*

In the following weeks I took up the offer from a professor at the local university to accompany him, for a decent honorarium—whatever that was supposed to mean in the case of this well-known cheapskate—to a historians' congress in Göttingen to prepare his new work (a collection of old essays) for publication. A trip designed to prepare me for life after Helga. I was to help create the impression that he had written a new book from scratch since this was the only way he could claim the full fee a second time over. What would have been acceptable as a collection of various essays and speeches written for different occasions and for very different audiences, was a disaster as a monograph. Every ten pages the same content came up in a slightly different form or with slightly different words, which meant that one understood the thin seam of thought but constantly wondered why it had to be repeated over and over again. While we sat side by side in the buffet of the express train and were carried across Germany, I highlighted the repetitions with a red pencil and we then worked to make them appear different by adding a few choice formulations here and there. In truth, I was only really thinking about my dog, who, after only a week with me, had done everything he could to stop me going away. I was supposed to stay at home, as would be right for a larger dog. So he lay down in front of the door and was not willing to let me leave the house. How was I to make it clear to the professor that the only way to prevent his already dubious professional reputation from being completely destroyed was to rewrite the whole thing, and, yes, I used that word. Rewrite? He looked at me askance—I had been thinking about the terrible yowling of the dog—as if I had just taken away his permission to teach. What do you mean? The book was about the fraught process of dissolving the state institutions during the last months of the GDR, but apart from the message that it was fraught there wasn't much to say, above all because the newspapers had covered it in exhaustive detail. While I gazed at the startled professor's bad teeth, as he sat there, mouth agog, I found myself thinking about my dog's wonderful teeth, and, instead of setting out the urgent changes required in the book, I told the poor man about the matte gleam of my dog's canine teeth and how he was waiting for me at home. Shortly before we arrived in Göttingen I had finished my account and I pictured, as the summation of our conversation, so to speak, the dog tearing into this manuscript with gusto and ripping it to shreds, like some tenacious predator, a talent he had already demonstrated with several of the more indigestible works of world literature. As I was shaving for this journey, the dog had found the second volume of a costly Achim von Arnim edition under the bookshelf—squarely in his territory therefore—and first reduced it to its component parts and then later into tiny pieces and sat there, work complete, with his incomparable doggy smile and challenged me to make a book out of it again. Can dogs smile? the professor asked.

In our hotel—one of those buildings that should have been torn down right after it was built—a message was waiting that I should ring Helga immediately. Oh my God, I thought, something has happened to the dog! But thanks to a merciful God it was nothing to do with the dog but Helga herself. She was pregnant, she whispered into the telephone, and, as it couldn't possibly be mine, I could ask quite innocently—after a pause—who the father was. The answer came after another pause, enough time for me to reflect that, if things kept going at this rate, the flat would soon be too small for our rapidly growing family. The dog had chosen the servants' room; Helga was lodging in the newly decorated guest room; my library was occupying the large living room and I had the small spare bedroom, in which I also worked. We ate in the kitchen. As I was steeling myself to hear the name Kurt at any second—Kurt who had had his way with the life and soul of his shabby 'Pfalzstube'—a word emerged from the telephone that despite the whisper in which it was uttered, carried a power that literally threw me to the floor: Christoph.

That miserable God-botherer with his crooked face, that freeloading slimeball, that bloody parasite living off the blissful ideal of Christianity, that Bible-bashing Pharisee, had dared to soften up the woman on the stairs with his fantasies about salvation and God had allowed it to happen.

And, I asked, do you love him?

I went through the essays with the professor, cutting and pasting even when it didn't really help; but we ended up striking the majority and turning the intended academic book into a slim essay, if one is allowed to use such high-flown words. The contemporary historian tested out the shortened version of his paper in the conference strand 'perspectives on future historiography' and was not even surprised by the positive reception. To celebrate his success, he bought me a glass of wine which, as he expressly remarked, he did not intend to deduct from the honorarium.

After this drink I went to the station. The restaurant was probably the only place in all of Göttingen where one wouldn't meet historians. I saw a female Jehovah's Witness and bought a copy of her apocalyptic newspaper; when she turned up in the restaurant later on, I invited her to join me for a meal. Her name was Halina: a confessing Catholic, hailing from the Balkans. Her three children had, as she said, got into trouble because of the lack of balance in their souls. We drank a bottle of Riesling together and ate Bockwurst while she described the storm that was threatening to break over us at any time. Let it come, I thought, and let Christoph be the first to feel it.

I cannot find the words to tell the outcome of this tragedy with a lightness that would make it bearable. I became a collector of shadows, walking all night long through the streets of Göttingen, until at last the first train departed that could deliver me to the epicentre of the disaster.

When I opened the door to my home, I was confronted immediately with the dramatic misery of my existence. The dog was not there. I had reckoned on Helga's absence. Shame would have made her slip away; but it had been beyond my worst imagining that Helga and the father of her child would have just upped and left with all her worldly goods. Her room had been emptied down to the last item and was so spick and span that it looked as if no one had lived there for years. She had taken the postcard from the table in the hall, a drawing of Botticelli's 'Paradise' that I had given her once, and there was a space where the catalogue of Dégas's drawings had been: one of the few books that she would look at regularly because she was fascinated by the strangely distorted bodies. She had even taken her soap with her. As was to be expected, the flat was perfectly tidy—only the woman and the dog were missing.

Three days later the dog, at least, returned. I answered the door and I could hear the dog rushing up the stairs, beside itself with pleasure. No idea who delivered it.

After a further three days there was an envelope with a black border lying in the post box. I felt my childhood fears rising in me because this was precisely the way that I received notice of the deaths of, first my parents and then, a few days later, my grandparents. All four of them died within a week.

Christoph had died, 'by his own hand', as it stated. The card was signed, in this order, by Kurt and Helga. 'We will not forget you', was printed on the card. Some people die because they have lived, others because they have not lived. How strange to read the name Helga on a death announcement.

When I was looking through the newspaper later, I even found Christoph's obituary; his significant contribution to theodicy was mentioned but also the 'Red Cell Theology' that he initiated in the 1960s and which had caused some uproar in church and academic circles. The attempt to drag God down to earth using violence was as ridiculous as it was wrongheaded; and because the Christian God, unlike Buddha, was not exactly known for his sense of humour, he punished the rebellious followers with contempt. In any case, his having founded the 'Red Cell Theology' was the motive for rejecting Christoph's professorial work on the problems of theodicy—for 'political reasons'. Maoism and theodicy. That was too much, even for academia, at that time.

On the day of the funeral—I had just about got back to work, dog at my feet—Kurt called to ask if I wanted to say a few words at the grave. No, I did not.

But I took the dog to the funeral, although dogs are not allowed in the cemetery. A handful of people stood around the grave. I saw Kurt and a few of the indefatigable drinkers from the 'Pfalzstube'. The poet Ewald Hartmann was there, trying to look, as ever, like Stefan George. His nose was so pointed that I once wrote in a review, over thirty years ago, that his poems felt as though they had been written with the tip of his nose, an allusion to Kafka, who said somewhere that a woman with only one tooth left in her mouth looked as though she might laugh with this one tooth. Hartmann's work consisted of a single long poem that he had been rewriting all his life, but the metaphysical élan with which he had started was by now used up. He had nothing more to say, literally, but was still a poet and could therefore open a slate with Kurt.

I didn't stay because the dog was pulling on the lead. There was no sign of Helga. Wandering around I met acquaintances who were burying a film director whom I thought had died long before. We once wrote a script together with which we wanted to revolutionize conventional film but we didn't get any financial support. Without state support it is impossible to revolutionize either film or society. The few friends wanted to invite me to the wake but I didn't go with them. 'Funeral feast', such a beautiful word: it must have been invented by crows.

I thought about a remark that Kurt had made on the telephone when I declined to hold a speech about Christoph. You're quite wrong about him, he said, after he had listened to my imprecations. Would I have to reproach myself with the fact that my unconscionable lack of feelings for the special nature of this failed theologian meant that I was partly responsible for his so-called voluntary death? No. We all wrote a lot of nonsense back then, but to doubt God's sovereignty because he hadn't stopped that which he could have, was something only Christoph would have been capable of. He was simply not equal to it. Anyway: the drinking that set in back then had nothing to do with me and why, in God's name, did he steal away my angel whom he was also not equal to?

It was good to show the dog the cemetery. We looked at all the graves of people I once knew. He was a writer, I said to the dog, who didn't write any longer; we once lived together in a house; this one was an actor who played a big role on TV but when it became known that he had AIDS was no longer employable. A mayor, a pub landlady, a cameraman. An actress who had died from taking too much coke. At some point I got the impression that the dog had lost interest in all the dead. For him, in comparison to the living, there were too many dead people.

So I went home with the dog and carried on correcting the world and improving it as well as I could.

And that is how I went on living.

THE GLASS EYE

My grandfather had one eye. The other was made of glass. When the smoke coming out of the tiny oven that heated our room affected him, he would take out his glass eye and put it down on the table in front of him. It always seemed to me that it was looking at me but, in truth, it was me looking at the glass eye.

Why do you have a glass eye? I asked him.

Because I can see inside with it, Grandfather answered. Everything inside is much bigger and richer than you think. He never said what he saw when he looked inside, and, because his eye socket closed up to a slit when the eye lay on the table in front of him, I couldn't check.

My grandfather did not know why he was still alive. He wrapped himself up in his sadness, like a coat.

Why am I still alive? he asked me again and again. I had no answer. Leave the boy alone, said Grandmother who thought such questions were foolish. One was alive because one was alive. But Grandfather wouldn't let it go. Sometimes, when his sadness had completely enveloped him, he would take me in his arms and we would cry together. Or, rather, I would sob and he would cry quietly to himself, and when I looked at his glass eye during what was, in truth, a reassuring ritual, I would see that, much to my relief, it was wet too. My grandfather could cry with both eyes, even though one of them was glass.

Why was one alive and why was there a moment in life where one no longer wanted to live? When the three of us sat together—Grandfather, Grandmother and me—there were not many questions. Not that questions were forbidden. But it seemed to me that the two old people were uncomfortable with having to provide answers. When I asked a question, instead of trying to find an answer, Grandfather would say: that is a difficult question. The world is just the way it is. You cannot change it by asking questions. One has to find answers for oneself, even if one is not asked to. What one did with these answers was up to the individual. So at some point I gave up asking about my parents. Everybody in the world has parents, I had grandparents. There was nothing more to say.

So, Grandfather didn't want to live any more. He had lived long enough and obviously experienced something that had taken away the pleasure of life. But what? It can't have been anything to do with Grandmother or me, because he was always friendly to us, so it must have had something to do with what he saw when he looked inside. When I shut my eyes and looked inside, I could see our village, the few animals that still lived on our farm, the dog, the sunken path, the quarry, all the paths I had walked with Grandfather, the old fruit trees, the thrushes and skylarks, and, of course, I saw Grandfather and Grandmother everywhere and I wished to myself that none of it would ever disappear. One of these things must have a secret hidden within that only Grandfather could see and that so upset him he didn't want to live any more.

During our ritual bouts of sadness, I would stand between Grandfather's knees while he sat on a chair by the window and put my arms around his neck so that our heads were touching, like horses. Because Grandfather had no money, he could only shave once a week which meant that six times a week it scratched when I put my arms round him. You should shave, Grandpa, I said to him, and he answered that there was no point any more. Yes, there is, I said, because then you won't be scratchy. He was too weak to explain the reasons to me. His inner desolation had grown so all-encompassing that in my mind I saw him passing through empty rooms in which even his inward-looking eye could see nothing at all. He was empty. While I could feel how life was pulsing inside me and wanted to get out, there sat opposite me an empty old man, who could no longer connect with his inner world. Once he told me that he only stayed alive because of me, not even because of Grandmother, and I had to promise him that I wouldn't tell her that. Without me there would be no point any more. He suspected Grandmother of having had private conversations with God and he didn't want to get involved. God would take care of Grandmother and that would leave only me.

If I believed him, there was no point to anything anymore. If you lost a tooth, there was no point in going to the dentist in town. If Grandma wanted to fix his jacket, it was not worth the trouble.

The only thing that was worth staying in the world for was me.

Sometimes, when he was looking out of the window with a particularly sad face, I asked him why he was so sad. It was to do with Russia and Hitler, he said, after a long pause, long enough to give me time to imagine Russia, but I was not allowed to talk to anyone about it, otherwise he would end up in prison. Not even with Grandma? Not even Grandma, not with anyone. Why Hitler, whom I sometimes heard talked about, and the vast country of Russia were responsible for Grandfather's sadness, was something he never explained. Hitler was responsible for lots of things, I understood that. But how the little man I saw in the paper had managed to be responsible for almost everything remained a mystery. And then Grandfather used the thick blue veins on the back of his hand to show me where Russia was and where he had been in Russia. That's the Volga, he said, and there's the Dnieper. There were no rivers in our village and my imagination ran riot. Wonderful rivers! Grandfather said. And there we were sitting in a wobbly little boat, him at the helm and me with a bucket in my ice-cold hands bailing out the water that came over the sides, the enemy in noisy gunboats behind us. We can hear their rough, throaty shouts telling us to surrender but Grandfather pulls the tiller hard and pushes on upstream, past the men and we can see their wide-open eyes and mouths and waving arms and before they can get to their rifles we are far out of sight in the thick Russian darkness, disappearing over the great river.

One day I found some rifles badly concealed in a quarry near our house. I often used to go to the quarry, although it was forbidden, but nobody in the village paid any attention. There were lots of rumours about the quarry. They said that there was a resistance movement but nobody spoke about what that actually meant. The last unit had fought there and those that didn't fall in battle were executed on the spot. But why? Hitler was responsible for that too, the little man with the moustache and the neatly trimmed hair. The rifles smelled good. A strange smell of machine oil and camphor. I found them under a broken elderberry bush, four of them, as good as new. Why had they left such valuable objects behind? I hung one of them around my neck and walked home past all the houses in the village. My grandmother nearly jumped out of her skin, and Grandfather started to shake when he held the rifle in his hand. Russian, he said, Cyrillic lettering! If anyone had seen you, it would have been really bad, but the few people in the village were out on the fields. I was not yet five years old and had already held a Russian rifle in my hand.

I slept in my grandparents' big bed, me in the crack in the middle, Grandmother next to the window. Both of them had a glass of water for their teeth on their bedside tables, and Grandmother also had a Bible, an illustrated version in which the history of the Jews was shown in dramatic pictures. Moses, for example, parting the Red Sea with a single wave of his hand, so the Jewish people could cross with dry feet. People couldn't swim back then, Grandmother said. That's why Moses had to intervene. I couldn't swim yet either but there wasn't a Moses in the village who could command the waters of the pond to make way. Once, I slid down the slope to the pond and broke through the ice, which gave me a nasty cut under the eye. I had to get myself out because there was no one there to save me. I got home wet and bleeding, and Grandmother got into bed next to me to warm me up and read me stories from the Bible. I found it difficult to grasp what the Jewish people had had to go through. All the trials that God, for whatever reason, laid upon them were pictured and so I suffered twice with them. The physical excitement I felt when I looked at the pictures only strengthened my feeling that there must be supernatural powers that have nothing to do with our poor little world. Above all, however, there was a world outside our village. There was Russia and there was Berlin, where my parents lived, and between them, the five parts of the world that the Jews had settled. I found it strange that they had left the warm, dry land by the Dead Sea, and Grandmother's explanation that Christ had sent them out into the world didn't convince me either. Christ could make water into wine, after all, and he could feed a whole people with one loaf of bread, so why didn't he just repeat his miracles there where he had grown up? The disciples, whose names I had learnt by heart and whose faces I had committed to memory, went out into the world to spread the gospel, Grandmother explained, and because they did that we are all now under God's protection. If God had not been holding his hand over you, you would have drowned just now. It is that simple. If only one could believe it!

The room the three of us lived in was just big enough for there to be space next to the bed for a sort of trunk for storing clothes and a table with three chairs. Grandfather's was covered in faded brown velvet. The velvet smelt so good! When Grandfather looked out of the window, I used to rub my nose along the velvet on the arms of the chair and breathe in deeply to taste all the subtleties hidden in this scruffy, soft material. Velvet! Even the word smelt good, like cinnamon. Grandmother had managed to save a little jar with cinnamon sticks; they were so precious that we never used them, just smelt them now and again. One day, when there was rice again, the cinnamon would come into its own they said; but when that day would be remained unclear, as did most other things. One day—how often I had heard those words.

Next to the window was a colour print hung on a nail; if there was bad weather, I would study it for hours on end. It showed a rising landscape and, in the background, on a hill, a large city, protected by towers like the water tower just outside our village that had been damaged by gunfire. The city was free Jerusalem. As if trying to protect the city, the painter had painted a double row of perfectly round trees that framed it. In the foreground were two shepherds in strange positions: one cloaked in a red cloth, and the other wearing a yellow waistcoat; and to the right and in front of them sat a man in a blue tunic, a book in his lap and a red hat on his head. He was pointing to the shepherds who were watching twelve sheep and a goat who all looked so peaceful that they didn't really need watching. Whenever I tore myself away from this heart-rending picture, and gazed out of window next to it, I felt utterly wretched, even if I couldn't find words to express that wretchedness. The difference between what was possible and what I experienced here on our farm was so clear and compelling that no further words were necessary. The painter had painted paradise but our farmyard, as Grandfather once said, had become hell. While, in the picture, the sheep grazed on the meadow, in our yard there was a broken handcart and rusted machines that no one thought to repair, and next to the dung heap they had built a slaughtering pen where the pigs were killed in the most brutal way and hung up to bleed. The horrified squealing of the pigs drove my grandfather to despair. They should be treated like that, the swine, he cried out, and Grandmother muttered that he shouldn't say such things in front of the child. The child was me.

I want to live there with you one day, I said to my grandparents, pointing to the beautiful city that towered in the background of the picture; and my grandmother pulled the faded curtains across the window so that we could all three of us gaze at it. Free Jerusalem!

'What do you want to be?' Grandfather asked.

'I want to be what you once were,' I replied.

There was a three-part folding screen between the trunk and the table, the most valuable piece of furniture in a room, designed more for dwarfs than normal people. It was made, my grandfather emphasized at every possible opportunity, out of a frame of the finest cherry wood and was covered with embroidered linen. There were the most extraordinary birds sitting on palm trees in some sort of jungle or hanging from vines in a world that, in my imagination, reminded me more of Moses than our farm. Grandfather was a talented birdsong imitator, and I only had to point to one of the birds to set him twittering. And in summer, when the window was open and the birds outside were singing, he would stage whole plays in bird voices in which the birds on the screen had put on costumes and pretended to come from far-off lands, about which they told the most impossible stories. In truth, behind the feathers of the parrot was an ordinary sparrow, and behind the toucan's costume nothing more than a song thrush. The sparrow could talk like a parrot and the thrush could squawk like a toucan. I had to make do with these extraordinary abilities while I knew that parrots really existed but in a quite different reality, and that toucans were real too and not merely the imaginings of the screen-maker. I became Columbus, discovering the New World: America, Asia, Africa and, my favourite, Australia where, as the parrot explained to me, animals carried their young in pouches on their stomachs. Europe became more and more pale. Europe was our village. Europe was the terrible things my grandfather had experienced in Russia, in the Soviet Union, as I always had to call Russia when I was not at home, so as not to 'draw attention to myself'; Europe was a shortage of chocolate and the absence of cinnamon and lemons, which were available in other parts of the world and even hung on trees along the roadside; Europe was the glaring injustice that my grandfather's farm had been taken from him and that we were now 'allowed' to live there, in one tiny room.

That meant, for example, that we no longer had access to my grandparents' old bathroom on the ground floor; something that caused my grandmother particular hardship. Not only was the hot water from the boiler no longer available to us, which meant we had to wash in a basin, I also had to carry the water upstairs in an old discarded milk churn. The bowl in which we washed was made of enamel, a word I loved. It was one of the few words that were particular to us—enamel and eiderdown—though the things that they signified were far from precious. The eiderdown was a lumpy feather bedspread and the enamel on the bottom of the bowl had broken off and left behind a strange pattern. When I had a cold, I had to bend over a hot herbal mixture with a towel over my head and could study the pattern long and hard. A blotch that was jagged in some places, then smooth, and changed when a drop of sweat fell into the water, before regaining its old shape a few seconds later. I recognized all the stories from the Bible that Grandma had read to me in this unsightly blotch; and sometimes, when I was quite overcome by the heat under the towel, the disciples would appear out of the water and invite me to join them in a meal at their big table.

What is that boy still doing under the towel, Grandfather asked when I showed no sign of emerging. He's getting well, said Grandmother.

We were also not permitted to use the toilet, which was a catastrophe for Grandfather because he had a weak bladder and had to pee in a bucket at night, which often led to spillages and, the morning after, to long complaints and confessions. It was humiliating for the pair of them that they had to do their business in an earth privy in the vegetable garden; something that didn't really bother me, as long as it wasn't the middle of winter. Particularly in spring I enjoyed sitting on the smooth wooden seat and thinking up stories about hell, the entrance to which I imagined just below me and into which I would cast everyone who had insulted my grandfather. It's not in itself such a bad thing to have to sit on a privy unless, of course, you have used a proper toilet with a flush.

I wasn't quite sure whether Adelheid should go to hell as well. Adelheid was the daughter of the administrator who had been put in place by the Soviet occupying power and of whom Grandfather said—'but never tell anyone I said this'—that he knew nothing about anything and sod all about farming. He sat, together with his companions, in what used to be our living room, drinking vodka out of my grandmother's Meissen china, and, when they wanted to go to the toilet, they went into Grandfather's bathroom and sat on the porcelain pan for as long as they wished.

When I was sent to fetch water I often met Adelheid on the stairs, as if she were waiting there for me. Come on, I'll show you something, she would say and then take me into the room where Grandmother's clothes hung on coat-hangers in her bulky wardrobes. She took off her grubby dress and put on one of my grandmother's; and in the time between taking off and putting on I was allowed to look at her. There wasn't a lot to be seen but there was enough to make me think that, beyond the continent I knew, there was another that would be rewarding to explore. I wasn't allowed to touch her, although she constantly asked me to do up a zip here or fasten some hooks there and once she put on one of grandmother's shapeless corsets which was so difficult to do up that she had to lie on the sofa so that I could work on it. There she was, lying naked before me like a newborn calf and fear constricted my throat because all I could think about was that, as I was kneeling on her trying to find the blasted eyelets, the door might open at any moment and Adelheid's mother would see the grandson of the expropriated farmer sitting, sweating, on her daughter's back. But her mother didn't come in. And when I had finally struggled the corset off again, Adelheid said, you can go now. My grandmother was waiting impatiently for me upstairs, wearing only her petticoat which she kept on when she was doing the washing. In contrast to Adelheid, my grandmother kept all the secrets of the human body out of sight.

Once, when I was standing on the stairs with the milk churn to catch my breath, the new administrator called me into my grandparents' old living room. He was lying stripped to the waist on our good sofa, with his dirty work shoes on, a bottle of vodka in his hand. He was speaking with two workers who used to be my grandfather's workers. One of them sat on the walnut sideboard, banging his legs against the wood. The other, a Communist, as grandfather told me later, was lounging in the big armchair next to the window. What has your grandfather been saying about me, the administrator asked. We never talk about you, I lied. If you are lying we will skin you alive, the Communist said, like a rabbit, and the other worker, who was sitting on the sideboard, laughed so loud that snot burst out of his nose and he wiped it on the top of the sideboard. Your grandfather is a traitor, he said, and I saw that he hardly had any teeth in his mouth. Ask your grandfather what he thinks of me, the administrator said, and then come back here and tell me. As he spoke he was cutting huge chunks of sausage with his pocketknife and shoving them, skin still on, into his mouth. Then he licked the knife with his tongue and stuck it into the living room table, where it stood, quivering. I had never seen such a big sausage.

My grandmother was very devout. She couldn't go to her own church any more, as it was being used to store agricultural implements—a sacrilege that took every ounce of this resolute woman's determination to endure—so our room was used as a church. We didn't have anything to do anyway.

On Sundays the three of us would sit together, at the table, singing hymns. Or rather, she sang, Grandfather hummed the bass notes and I moved my lips. We prayed before and after the hymns. When we got to the part 'and give us this day our daily bread', I stole a glance at Grandfather who, in turn, gazed at the empty breadbasket, with a worried, sad look on his face. The scene was characterized by a strange solemnity, strange because we had to be constantly thankful for something that we didn't have. How are you supposed to believe in a God whose behaviour is so distant, even parsimonious? Our church had an important trial in store for me.

Alongside these official ceremonies there was another, quite different, religious practice that was much more disturbing. It took place at night, away from prying eyes. I always had to go to bed first and was kissed and hugged as if I were going abroad for years and it was doubtful whether I would return. Of course, I didn't go straight to sleep, but strained to catch the voices of the old couple as they discussed all the worries they didn't want to burden me with during the day. They occasionally talked about my parents, about the struggle to get enough to eat, about lawsuits that Grandfather wanted to bring but which Grandmother talked him out of, about the American zone, about relatives that were missing or dead, and, of course, about the bloody regime and how it was ruining the farm. Occasionally Grandfather would switch on the People's Radio to listen to the news but the propaganda just led to even deeper hopelessness. This room was not made for the world that was described in the news. Every night the same words: I'm going to bed! Then he would come around to my side of the screen, take off. his trousers with a sigh and lie down in bed in his shirt and underclothes after dropping his teeth into the glass of water with a gurgle. Grandmother would keep playing her game of patience, which she played with a set of the original Altenburg playing cards that Grandfather said had gone Communist too, until she heard the deep, archaic snoring, as Grandfather bid goodbye to the injustices of the visible world. At that moment she would also come to our side of the screen, take off her dress and put on her nightshirt, remove a couple of clips from her thin hair, which she then brushed a few times, put her teeth in a water glass and slipped under the eiderdown, always careful not to wake up either of 'her men'.

And then began the séance, which always made my heart beat so loud that I was afraid she would hear it. She began by asking her very busy God, 'in these difficult times', to pay her a little attention because she had something very important to tell him. When she was certain that he was listening—and I was sure that he wouldn't be able to ignore her pleading voice—she suddenly began, with no further ado to 'pick a bone with him'; by which I mean that she started on the most bitter reproaches, then hissed a volley of complaints and oaths until her voice broke and she took up the gentle tone with which she had begun. It came down to the same thing: God should make more of an effort or he would lose her, one of his most loyal followers. To placate him she always added a final sentence, one that literally made the blood run cold. 'I thank you, Lord, she whispered, that you have sent us this grandson. We will always be grateful'.

Sometimes I had the feeling that God would not put up with this treatment: I was scared, particularly when the window was open, that he might arrive in person to read Grandmother the riot act, an expression that Grandfather liked to use when anger came upon him between two bouts of sadness. But God did not appear, the riot act wasn't read and at some point we must all have fallen asleep.

We never had visitors, with two exceptions. Sometimes the dog Grandfather had known in earlier times would drop by. He was so old that it took an eternity for him to pant his way up the stairs to our room. If he met anyone on the stairs he would get a kick, but he was too old even to bark. He's going to visit the class enemy, the administrator would say, if he saw the animal crawling up the stairs, he'll get some nice chops. But the dog was so weak that he couldn't even imagine chops any more. He scratched at the door until he was let in, upon which he was received like an old King and keeled over more or less straightaway. There he would lie, gazing up with his old eyes, as grandfather told stories about the adventures they had had. They were very old friends. I lay next to the dog on the floor, my head on his stomach because I wanted to hear his heart and was sometimes not sure whether he understood my Grandfather.

The other visitor was a Polish man who, according to Grandfather, had lost his mind. He used to work for my grandfather but now lived in the forest. You could see that from the skin on his hands and face, which was always bloody and scratched. He passes through the brambles like a saint, my grandmother would say; then she would set to work with her herbal tinctures. He would only come when he could be sure that nobody would see him; he would suddenly appear in the room, covered in blood and trembling all over. After he had been treated he would sit, stock-still, on my chair for a couple of hours without saying a word until he toddled off again. He brought us mushrooms wrapped in his handkerchief and berries that were difficult to find. You have to be very kind to him, Grandmother said, and because I didn't know what else to do, I stood behind him and rested my hand on his shoulder.

The first thing Grandfather did in the morning was to smoke a pipe. On the wall behind his chair there always hung a tuft of brown leaves given to him by one of his few remaining friends. He would tear one off like the page of a calendar and cut it into tiny pieces with the knife he also used to eat. He scrunched the pieces together with spit until they fitted into his pipe. When I looked at our window from the farmyard in winter the windowpane seemed opaque. It was too cold in our room so the window was very rarely opened. The smoke clung to everything, especially the blankets and our clothes, which went against the grain for Grandmother, but in this she was powerless. The pipe was Grandfather's anchor in life; if he had been forbidden to smoke he would have died on the spot.

If the weather was amenable we would go 'hunting for food', as Grandfather called it. Until the expropriation of his land he had been the 'potato man' in his area, a position that earned him respect and he was constantly asked for advice about the characteristics of different soil types. He knew everything there was to know about potatoes and could describe every tuber with an endless patience. He would break the potato in two with his thumb, lick the exposed parts and begin a lecture which would often expand into the history of the potato. He spoke with such enthusiasm that it might almost have been him that had gone to America, discovered the potato and cultivated it. He raved about sweet potatoes that tasted of marzipan and floury potatoes for animals, about salted potatoes and about a hundred different ways of making potato broth. The idea that the potatoes in our area would not grow to their full size nor develop their unique taste, because of agricultural mismanagement made him so sad that sometimes, holding the broken tuber in his hand, he would be lost for words and I would have to nudge him so that he came back down to earth from his potato heaven. We don't know anything about the world, he would say sometimes, and that is good and bad. If we knew everything we would not be able to live, he explained, but, for example, if we knew nothing about potatoes we would be much the poorer for it.

But my grandfather was also an expert on herbs and berries, mushrooms and edible plants. If we went hunting for food, we would come back with a big bag full of treasures that would then have to be sorted and cut, washed and dried. Beechnuts, hazelnuts, blackberries and elder, young nettles, a thousand different herbs, camomile, wild oats and wild garlic, field flowers from which he could make tea or poultices for his tired bones: almost everything could be used if you knew how. He could make capers out of the pistils of marsh marigolds; he would conjure up a ragout from supposedly inedible mushrooms that was so good that it could have graced the menus of the best restaurants in the world.

If we passed little farms or houses while we were out on our walks, we would often be asked into the kitchen or even into the parlour. I was amazed how people looked up to him—this man who was scarcely acknowledged on his own farm. Often he was treated like a hero, but not a home-spun potato hero, a proper hero.

I didn't understand anything the grown-ups talked about; there were a few individual words that ran around in my head, took root and grew into fantastical stories in which Grandfather, with his glass eye, was the saviour of Saxony and had defended our land against the Russians.

On the way home I was allowed to open the old newspaper bags that our neighbours had given us to take away. Sometimes there was an egg, sometimes some bacon or even a piece of cake, sometimes a little jar of marmalade or a big, thick mustard gherkin. To me these were a kind of homage to my important grandfather.

Back home, I would ask Grandmother why Grandfather was worshipped as a hero and why people made such offerings to him.

Grandmother answered laconically: what sort of stories has he been telling you this time?

So I went to Grandfather and asked him: Grandfather, were you a hero?

He had his evil-smelling pipe in his hand, from which a rope of thick, dark smoke rose up that almost enveloped him. I stood in front of him and tried to look into him through his glass eye. He said nothing. He looked at me for a long time and was silent. A peaceful silence. Neither of us had noticed that the tatty curtains had caught fire and that smouldering scraps of cloth were falling onto his shoulders and the brown velvet of his chair before floating down onto the rag rug; the window frame was already ablaze, the glass burst and crashed into the room, where the clothes trunk, the screen and the bed were soon burning too. The birds on the screen screeched and tried to escape through the open window, their plumage already burning; now the flames had reached Grandmother's dress and she stood in the middle of the room like a life-size torch, her hair a wreath of fire, the burning Bible in her outstretched hand.

It was as silent as the grave.

My childhood was over.